Go When You

See the Green Man

Walking

Christine Brooke-Rose

Go When You

See the Green Man

Walking

Christine Brooke-Rose

Verbivoracious Press

Glentrees, 13 Mt Sinai Lane, Singapore

This edition published in Great Britain & Singapore

by Verbivoracious Press

www.verbivoraciouspress.org

ISBN: 978-981-09-2167-5

Printed and bound in Great Britain & Singapore

First published in Great Britain by M. Joseph, 1970.

Contents

Introduction:

The Eye and the Word

JOANNA WALSH

The first story in *Go When You See the Green Man Walking*, 'George and the Seraph', opens with an eye. Someone is looking not through, but onto the eye. "My blue eye, which was myself, blinked again into wavelengths that suddenly rippled with laughter", and the image vanishes. The speaker is the possessor of the eye, who, as a seraph, is only occasionally embodied, and looks, (from the perspective of what?) simultaneously onto, and through his (her, its?) occasional physical functions. At first it's quite difficult for the reader to orient her (him?) self in relation to the narrator, and the subjects, and objects he (she? it?) is seeing. "Naturally," says the seraph, "it's all an optical illusion. There is nothing here but a large dark vacuum."

The difficulties of the eye are at the centre of Brooke-Rose's stories, and she addresses them in her book of essays, *Invisible Author*. "The difficult thing I have been doing on and off for the last thirty-six years," she wrote in 2002, "has a technical name, a lipogram, though I'd prefer the word constraint . . . a refusal of the narrative past tense." Consequent upon this constraint is a rejection of the literary historical present with its prescient closure—"It has to say 'then' for 'now', 'there' for 'here', 'the next day' for 'tomorrow'[1]"—and its author/narrator's omniscient

---

1 *Invisible Author*, Ohio University Press, 1 Jan 2002, p.134.

perspective.

The conventional literary solution to this problem has, Brooke-Rose writes, been the use of Free Indirect Discourse which implies an inner monologue while preserving all the privileges of third party narration (e.g. "He walked . . . would he find courage?[2]"), but this does little more than shift the problem. Can this voice be identified with the author, or does this technique give rise, as Brooke-Rose believes, to the idea of an omniscient, but responsibility-free, anonymous narrator. "Nobody speaks[3] here," (she quotes linguist, Émile Benveniste), "events seem to narrate themselves".

Instead, Brooke-Rose embraced the methods developed by Nouveau Roman writer, Nathalie Sarraute, one of the "true realists . . . who look so hard at a changing reality that they have to invent new forms."[4] Brooke-Rose was particularly influenced by the forms created by Sarraute's contemporary, Alain Robbe-Grillet, who used the third-person present tense, she says, like a "camera" (he had previously worked as an engineer) and "never evokes an act of seeing or consciousness . . . there is no see, only the seen"[5]. In her stories Brooke-Rose, like Robbe-Grillet avoids the parentheticals characteristic of Free Indirect Discourse ("he said", "she walked"), to create "the linguistic paradox of the technically authorless Narrative Sentence, freed from the speakerless state by the use of Speech Modes to narrate as 'I' (fairly common) or (very uncommon) remaining speakerless"[6]. "I took over," says Brooke-Rose, in *Invisible Author*, "and I hope extended, Robbe-Grillet's paradoxical use of a speakerless present tense of narrative."

"Who is speaking?" wrote Roland Barthes, quoting Beckett, in his essay, 'Death of the Author'. Brooke-Rose, who counted members of the OuLiPo and Tel Quel amongst her friends and colleagues, and who held a post in the literature department of the University of Paris Vincennes at the same time as Barthes was teaching at the Sorbonne, was concerned

---

2 *Ibid*, p.143.
3 *Ibid*. p.134.
4 *Ibid*., p.40.
5 *Ibid*., p138.
6 *Ibid*., p.134.

"with the whole question of the so-called death of the author and the author's authority"[7].

This idea translates fairly literally in the *Green Man* stories, many of whose narrators are, if not actually dead, disembodied, abstract, incomplete, mutable, or ill. In 'On Terms', a ghost haunts a landscape that is ghostly, the "vampiric jaw" of a Regency crescent where her ex-lover still lives with his wife. She waits outside his house, remembering, or is she experiencing for the first time: "Have you ever stood he says once when we are still on terms"? This Schrödinger's cat of a narrator, who may be dead, or may be still living, if only just, on one final trip after overdosing in her rented bedsit, is, understandably tense. Lacking the boundaries of punctuation, she's confused by what is past and what is present. "Like any constraint," wrote Brooke-Rose in *Invisible Author*, "the present tense is a limitation, but one that allows greater concentration on one aspect, simultaneity". Time cycles; the (possible) ghost haunts her lover's street with "my repeated presence". Brooke-Rose was bilingual, a native speaker of both French and English. I think of the French verb, *ressentir*, which ties memory to sensation (and, doing so, points up their Cartesian difference, perhaps). Sensations are recognised because they have been experienced before. "There are ways to recreate distress," says the patient's phantom limb that is the narrator of 'The Foot'.

The *Green Man* stories are full of repeat phrases that serve to anchor the passage of a being through time, and also of a being through the body, which it seems to live beside and, though affected by it, touches upon it only at intervals. How does the mind know it is in the body? Mostly, in these stories, by its aches and pains, and by their expression —the body is a symptom, both of itself, and of consciousness, which it in turn partially controls. "You are cherishing your symptoms my dear," says Mr. Poole, the seductive surgeon in 'The Foot'. "And are you occupying your mind?" Well, there's a question. Who, in Brooke-Rose's writing, consistently can?

The floating, narrative I of 'George and the Seraph', which is also, if

---

7 *Ibid*, p.14.

only sporadically, an eye, so insistent, and yet so absent, tells us that wherever there is somebody to look at, there must also be an 'I' to be looking. And eye is a feminist issue. Used to being evaluated by their looks, the eye affects the 'I' of women differently. "The victim to be haunted is female," says the phantom limb that narrates 'The Foot', using a telling passive construction. "It is also important," Foot says, "that the victim is beautiful." Before her accident, the patient was a model, and her looked-over body has given her the "habit of confidence", which makes Foot's job of creating the ghost of physical pain a challenge, but the patient's involvement with beauty is also her weak spot. "I knew then that the visioerotic element of her inner eye would always help me despite her intelligence or perhaps because of".

"It's best to haunt the intelligent," says Foot. "They are not used to responding fully with their bodies and the shock is greater." The (nameless) patient's intelligence manifests by her ability to tie ideas together: "She winds me round with other thoughts like boring details of hospital routine that loom larger than life or intrinsic worth and wrap each phantom fibre of me like a medullary sheath at times". In Brooke-Rose's stories, the body is seldom experienced cheerfully (an exception might be the body caressed by clothes in 'Go When You See the Green Man Walking') and it is not a path to liberation, but a constraint, a restraint, at best an illusion. Sicknesses of the body, or of the mind, are present in most of the stories, even if only in the background. In 'Red Rubber Gloves', one telling reference to "my relapse" (physical, mental? we're not told) immediately complicates the narrator's authority. But Brooke-Rose is not at heart a gothic, a sci-fi, or a horror writer. If her work contains elements of these genres, it is down to her mistrust of what manifests in the flesh. Several of the stories ('They All Go to the Mountains Now', and 'Medium Loser and Small Winner')—avoiding the "he said" "she said" parentheticals proscribed by Robbe-Grillet—consist almost entirely of dialogue.

Words may be a way out of the body.

"As a matter of fact," says the patient in 'The Foot', "I thought, perhaps, I could write."

"Oh yes," replies the "sexy-eyed" surgeon, "Love stories you mean? Or spies?" but no, she means a translation of her pain into words. "She is thinking of me to write about in order to get me out of her system as they call it," says Foot, "not sympathetic or parasympathetic autonomous but cerebrospinal out of her midbrain on to paper instead of aching there fifty-three and a half centimetres away from her stump." Words may trump flesh, but they are double-edged. "Nice word, intractable," says Foot, "in view of the way we phantoms infiltrate ourselves down the pathways of pain, down the spinothalamic tract to be precise, not that I'm partial to words, they can be enemies too, but I like words that bring alive my task my journey down the pathways of pain."

The phantom Foot is neuter, so far as we know, but falls for his 'victim'. Could Foot be male? Heterosexual seduction (usually via conversation) is Brooke-Rose's paradigm. The patient in 'The Foot' is patronised, and flattered by Mr Poole. Barely compensated-for by same-sex friendships, heterosexual romance is almost the only relationship played out in these stories, with the genders so polarised that the lovers are also always enemies. Brooke-Rose, who self-mockingly labelled her sexual/intellectual partners "mentowers[8]", concluded, in her fictionalised autobiography, *Remake* that she, like the narrator of 'Troglodyte', who ends up serving the man to whom she also pays rent, was on the whole better off without them.

Many of Brooke-Rose's male characters are doctors, or lay claim to their diagnostic privileges, but the sickness of the doctor is also always a possibility: "Why don't you go and eat?" says the Scent Maker to his exhausted and eccentric acupuncturist, the eponymous Needle Man. "I like it when it hurts," says the Needle Man, as he sticks pins into the Scent Maker's buttocks. Like Foot, the Needle Man is there to produce a physical effect but, as in 'The Foot', suffering is a flexible power relationship. The man in 'On Terms' says to his ghost stalker that he'd "got the impression you rather enjoyed" suffering. "Suffering," Queenie (fat, then thin) tells her doctor 'friend', is how she lost all that weight and became a celebrity spiritual guru. Spurious or not (and, as the

---

8 *Remake*, Carcanet Press, 1996, p.53, "The old lady is long past needing mentowers."

doctor/narrator is anything but trustworthy, who's to say that Queenie isn't the real thing) the spiritual is opposed to the flesh, and also to the 'I' (and, perhaps, therefore to the eye). Brooke-Rose, brought up nominally Catholic, though she claims it never took, said, in conversation with Lorna Sage[9], "The most important [religions] advocate annihilating the self in favour of Nirvana, God, thy neighbour, the other, and though none of us succeed in doing that, I believe it's the only important teaching. It's just possible that women have always been slightly better at it because they always have to follow a new clan and learn its language," language being, here, directly linked to authority.

The seraph, in the opening story, uses such earthly language that at first I'd expected the narrator might be George. It (he? she?) employs qualifiers—"of course", "I myself" "certainly"—that tell the reader there are some standards to be adhered to, but simultaneously imply the opposite: that—unreliable—they need to be constantly reaffirmed. They suggest to us that the seraph, and Foot, are not final authorities but psychological (or spiritual) middlemen; we never glimpse their own watchmen. Perhaps language itself is in control and, if so, what hope is there for either its perpetrators or its victims?

The last, and title, story in the collection, is perhaps Brooke-Rose's most successful experiment with Robbe-Grillet's third person, present tense "speakerless" narrative voice. A foreign woman (though we identify with her, and, instead, feel her setting's strangeness) buys a new, expensive suit that becomes her: "It is difficult in a strange country," says the mysterious, elegant woman who takes her shopping (an angel, a seraph?), "Or perhaps difficult always yes? You make mistakes? They hang in cupboard not put on for years?" Nevertheless, the woman makes a choice. "It's a good buy says the elegant foreign lady you will not regret." The language of clothes as the shrouds of identity has already been explored in 'The Religious Button', and 'Queenie'. In 'On Terms', the ghost lover is "acting out a fantasy that I can wear my temporal body and move about as if I existed." Clothes are only a step away from a phantom limb, and can be put on, or off, with similar ease or dif-

---

9 *Invisible Author*, p.176

ficulty.

The woman in 'Go' watches from her hotel window. She sees the green man, who tells her when to stop and when to go, when to return, and within what boundaries to walk. The woman watches a prostitute, who is eyed up by the passing men, though she does not look like a prostitute, but is "scholastic" in a prim navy skirt. The woman in the hotel room "opens the wardrobe and with a screech of agony her image vanishes." She puts on her new clothes, "She stands and sees a stranger framed in the strange room itself in the strange city. She opens the cupboard, the stranger screams and vanishes . . . She looks at the stranger who is beautiful." The woman in turn descends from her hotel in her expensive getup, to feel the caress of its silk, and of the gaze of the men on the street. A man flashes her. "She inclines her head politely to thank the man for the display." All Brooke-Rose's themes are there: authority, control, identity, body, vision, choice. "One could walk miles and miles," says the narrator, "obeying the code."

And, if one does not obey?

In her essay on gender and experimental writing, 'Illiterations', Brooke-Rose claims there is no space for a woman within the traditional parameters of creative practice. "All she can be is beautiful, and hence not understand beauty," or create it. Like Foot's patient she must, by force of necessity, write experimentally, which is the only way to defeat, to control, to get past the problem of the eye, which is also the problem of the 'I' and, especially for women, the body.

"Nathalie Sarraute[10]", says Brooke-Rose in 'Illiterations', might have "reversed the realist/formalist opposition and said that the true realists were those who look so hard at reality that they see it in a new way and so have to work equally hard to invent new forms to capture the new reality," but, "today one would push it much further and say, not that new ways of looking necessitate new forms, but that experiment with new forms produces new ways of looking, produces in fact the very story that it is supposed to reproduce, or, to put it in deconstructive terms, repeats an absent story."

---

10 *Stories, Theories, and Things*, Cambridge University Press, 1991, p.260.

Go When You See the Green Man Walking was first published in 1970, the heyday, perhaps, of literary theory as practice. 'Illiterations' was published in 1991, and *Invisible Author*, in 2002. "Difficulty," wrote Brooke-Rose, in those "Last Essays", "has now become unfashionable . . . the pleasure of recognition being generally stronger than the pleasure or puzzlement of discovery". Contemporary writers, she thought, had constructed a "blur" (a tellingly visual metaphor) that gives writing the "illusion" of being easy. "It's as if literary people didn't want their subject tarnished with difficult thinking," said Brooke-Rose in her interview with Sage, "But it'll come back. It always does. In a renewed form—like everything." Perhaps now is the time to begin to appreciate the nature of Brooke-Rose's achievement.

"Let us play," as she wrote, in *Stories, Theories, and Things*, "there are more theories in heaven and earth . . .[11]"

---

11 *Ibid.*, p.40.

George and the Seraph

So this is the Point of No Return. It doesn't look too bad, at least I can sit on it. At the other end I usually stand, but this is a special occasion, and I was told it is very like the other end, at least in essence.

There's certainly nowhere else to sit—just one big empty space. That's how it should be, of course. People always think that once they have reached this place and made the decision not to return everything will crowd in on them, exciting things like trees jiving and very fast cars with television windscreens so that they won't have to look ahead or in the rear mirror. That's why they come here, because everything will crowd in on them so that they cannot return, even if they lose heart at the last moment and want to. They call this making a decision.

Naturally, it's all an optical illusion. There is nothing here but a large dark vacuum. In fact it has to be a vacuum in order to give people the feeling that they are caught up in all those things and cannot return. If there really were a lot of things the people would be quite capable of turning away: you can always refuse something you see; it's what you imagine you see which is so difficult to forego.

The vacuum, moreover, makes them feel very light, like men in space-suits, floating around their rockets beyond the pull of gravity; they certainly look as clumsy, and in fact they plod as heavily as in a nightmare. But they feel airy and good. I myself am as light as an angel —well, lighter, actually, being a seraph—and I sit on the Point of No Return without even stretching it. Mind you, if they could see me, they would feel tremendously heavy, heavier even than they actually are— that's the effect I have on people, because I'm made of light.

But they cannot see me. They come up to the Point of No Return, inside this large dark vacuum, and the vacuum is divided into two seemingly limitless air-pockets, as if the sky behind them were a vast rubber holder gripping a mirror. They come up to this mirror and see all those exciting new things crowding in on them: there is a man selling coloured balloons, and each balloon is like a fortune-teller's crystal with things happening inside, such as rockets piercing the clouds and making them cry, and Venus languorous on the telephone to Mars, and a Japanese lawyer selling safe volcanoes on the moon to a land-speculator from Pompeii, smartly tailored in lava; there is a large hearse with a loudspeaker, racing through the streets like a police car, calling on everyone to vote for the new dead body; then another loudspeaker comes up and their two horns meet each other's huge lips and kiss with rude jazz noises and the crowd grows wild; there is an old lady trailing a fiery jet stamped Book of the Month and shouting I was Earth's First Human Satellite. Oh yes, there are plenty of exciting things to see in the mirror, so exciting that the people get caught up in them and cannot return. The mirror is, for the duration of my guard, myself, and I watch them come up to me and stare, and walk through me into the other side of the large vacuum, where all those new things are, when they have made the decision to go beyond the Point of No Return.

Not that the vacuum in front of me is completely dark: the mirror throws quite a bright gleam, even if it flickers a bit. Nor is it completely bare of things. All the way up to the Point of No Return, for instance, little scraps of paper are scattered through the dusk, all screwed up like flowers about to bud, and when you open them, they all have the same message hurriedly scrawled across them: *I will return*. These are signed variously, General McArthur, Jesus Christ, Billy the Kid, the Wandering Spring, the Flying Dutchman, the Great Mother, Hitler, and so on. The people pick them up and wear them in their buttonholes, and look like wedding guests.

Yesterday, George came along. Now I'm very fond of George. I know him well, from the other end, where I usually stand guard. And the reason why I'm very fond of George is that he believes in making Returns. 'There's no Point,' says George, 'in no Return.'

So that when he arrives at the Point he looks hard into the big screen and when he sees all those exciting new things that crowd in on you so that you cannot return, he scratches his head in a puzzled way and says 'It's all the same to me', which of course it is, because the big screen is only a mirror. And he goes back where he came from and starts all over again. I know this because the other end, where I usually stand guard, is much the same (at least in essence) as the Point of No Return, so that whatever goes on here is known at the other end even if I am not here. And of course I have seen him come back and start all over again many times, from the other end, where I stand guard since the genesis of things.

Most people think George is rather simple.

'There's no point,' said George again yesterday, 'in No Return.'

He stayed rather longer than usual, talking to one of the gardeners who look after the flowery scraps of paper.

'Most people seem to disagree with you, sir,' the gardener said, pointing his shaggy eyebrows and his pruning knife at the many wedding guests who were stumbling through me in the dark, past the Point of No Return.

'Most people think me rather simple,' said George, 'and I expect I am. I try very hard, and I come here often, but I just cannot see any difference between the things there and the things here. Except for the flowers. I don't think there are any flowers over there.'

He picked a scrap of paper and unscrewed it. *I will return*, it said, signed *The Unknown Warrior*.

'I like that,' said George, and put it in his buttonhole. This was the first time George had got as far as picking and wearing a flower, and I became a little alarmed, as he now looked very much like one of the many wedding guests who were stumbling through me in the dark. Usually he prefers just to look at the flowers.

'It's not a very successful one, that,' the gardener said. 'The trouble was, one of the sub-gardeners forgot which seed he had planted there, so that the poor flower struggled up without a name—I mean, it had one, of course, but we didn't know it, and none of these returning plants flourish with an Unknown Name.'

'Well I like it,' said George. 'After all, I also know very little. Don't you think it suits me?'

He preened himself a bit, looking into me without seeing me or beyond, and the gardener nodded politely.

'Do you ever try and cross any of these signatures?' George asked as he sat down between two flowers. 'For instance, a Wandering Jew with a Billy the Kid, that would make a powerful flower.' George was in a chatty mood.

'They've all been crossed hundreds of times,' the gardener replied, shaking his head with disapproval. 'To the point of exhaustion. At first it was healthy, the best with the best, or the weakest with the strongest, or red with blue, but now it's incestuous, at least, in the leading families. Why, there's hardly an original signature here, look at the handwriting. That's why the view is so much more confusing across there.' He waved his pruning knife in my direction.

George got up and peered through my huge blue eye until it blinked itself into great arpeggios climbing up and down guitar strings, like telegraph wires seen from a moving train. But the disturbance was only temporary, which was just as well, because it was rather painful.

'Perhaps I ought to go on after all,' George murmured, 'it does look a little different now.'

I was so surprised that my blue eye, which was myself, blinked again into wavelengths that suddenly rippled with laughter.
George looked up at the gardener and laughed too.

He laughed because he saw why the gardener laughed. Of course it looked different if one looked at it differently. And the gardener laughed because he knew that George liked coming here too much to go beyond the Point of No Return. George did not believe in No Return. So they both laughed.

Then they stopped laughing, and my ripples disappeared, because the women arrived, fussing as usual with their pots and ointments. And the women were weeping, just like the clouds pierced by the rockets inside the balloons sold by the man on the other side of me, and my enormous eye, which was myself, filled with one enormous tear, which was me, more transparent than ever, with more and more new things to be seen: a doctor rushing round with a big syringe, squirting bright red liquid on tall white walls and exclaiming, It works! It works! and the red liquid making exquisite designs like ideograms, which then took wing and filled the sky like locust-hordes and flew straight into the open mouth of a giant radio telescope that swallowed them up and swivelled away, then teleprinted them out over the tape-like streets until they became characters in a film crowd scene. So much was happening beyond me that the people poured in, delighted to be caught up in all those new things, and be unable to return. They did not notice the women, or George, or the gardener, they were so busy picking the flowers and putting them in their buttonholes, so as to look like wedding guests before rushing on into me.

But George saw only the women, who were weeping and fussing as usual with their pots and ointments, for the dead warrior, they said.

'After all,' George said to them patiently, 'the Warrior was Unknown, wasn't he! Why all this fuss with ointments?'

'Well, it helps the flower to grow next time,' the gardener explained. 'It's a perennial, you know.'

'Which way did he go?' the women asked.

'That way,' said the gardener, pointing to George's lapel, in which the flower was stuck. And the women were puzzled, because they expected the Unknown Warrior to look different, and not like George at all.

'He was more like the gardener last time,' said one of the women, who wore very high heels and black hair dyed reddish blonde a long time ago. Just like a golden sunset, George thought, fleeing from the growing night. And he was pleased with this thought. And because he was pleased with this thought he liked the woman whose hair had occasioned it, and smiled at her and her companions, so that there was a feeling of friendliness among them.

'Look, the gardener has gone,' the reddish blonde exclaimed. And so he had, almost as swiftly as the ripples in my enormous eye when his laughter stopped. 'He must have vanished when I mentioned his likeness to the Warrior.' And the women were puzzled again.

George was not surprised, because he knew that the gardener was a busy man, with the continuity of all those signatures to look after. The flowers were being continuously picked. Besides, it had happened before. George was not one to take offence, on the contrary, he was happy that the gardener had stayed so long just to talk to him.

He was about to show the women where he had picked the flower, when a noise like a plucked double bass, crescending, made him turn round. It was a rhythm of hoofs on the soft turf, bringing up four riders, jazzily dressed as in a musical Western, one in white, on a white horse, one in tan, on a sorrel horse, one in black, on a black horse, and one in buff, on a buff horse. And from the right hip of each straight trunk there stuck out a gun like a pollarded branch, and each right hand hovered over it as if to shelter it from my piercing gaze. They looked most picturesque, and behaved accordingly.

'Which way did he go?' they all asked together.

'Thattaway,' I said, jerking my thumb behind me.

For at this moment I had a thumb, a whole body in fact, at least to them, and to the women, and to George, and they could all see me. The women suddenly felt so heavy they could hardly walk. And the horses could not go forward, their legs were unliftable and their riders weighed like lead. And George was flat on his face, unable to move.

But I was still as light as an angel—well lighter actually, being a seraph.

The people were still coming up, and picking the flowers and walking into me in order to get caught up in all those new exciting things beyond me, so as not to have to return. They took no notice of the riders, or the women, or George. Perhaps they couldn't see them. They certainly couldn't see me, or they would also have been unable to move.

The riders recovered first, then the women, much more slowly. After all, this happens all the time, and they should know by now what to expect. The riders and their horses, whose colours came back gradually, moved painfully on through me, and the women followed, singing *Turn again Whittington*, I think, or something similar—anyway it sounded very much like bells. The people beyond me still couldn't see them, because they were so busy getting caught up so as not to have to return. And the women walked among them, singing, or chiming maybe. It was as if the vacuum had swallowed them up, or perhaps I did, for they all felt very heavy. But I was still as light as an angel—well, lighter actually.

George, however, remained in front of me, alone in the big empty space.

'I can't move,' he said. 'I can't go back. Does it mean I have to go on?'

'No, George,' I said very gently, so as not to frighten him. 'You can move. You can go back if you choose. Back to the beginning.'

'But that was yesterday,' he groaned.

'And now it's tomorrow' I replied. 'You can get up. It's light.'

'So it is,' said George. He got up, blinking, and stretched himself. 'It's dazzling.'

'That's only me,' I said modestly, 'and I'm only a reflection of the beginning.'

'I think I'll go on beyond the Point, now,' George said. 'I want to find the Unknown Warrior. I lost my flower during all that commotion, you know.'

'You do that, George,' I said softly. 'But come back, won't you?'

'Oh yes,' he said, moving lightly away from me, away from the Point of No Return, on which I was still sitting, and back to the beginning where he came from. 'It's only a mirror, after all,' George said as he looked over his shoulder, watching himself walk beyond the Point of No Return, 'and this way I can come back. I will return,' he called out as he waved at himself, and me.

When the gardener came back he found a new bud sprouting a small screwed-up paper which grew very fast under his gaze and blossomed out. It was picked by one of the many people who wanted to look like wedding guests before they rushed on through me, and it read I will return, signed George.

On Terms

The crescent street he lives in curves like a giant vampire's jaw, each house a long and yellow tooth, with the identical porches forming a second row. And in the last weeks of my life the street has certainly sucked my blood. I can still see and feel myself hiding behind the pillar in the last porch on the left which belongs to the rich old lady's house or after nightfall lurking among the trees of the semi-circular gardens that face the crescented houses. Watching him come and go. On my way to the office and again on my way home I stand behind the pillar of the last house for as long as time in my real life allows, and the rich old lady once or twice comes out and smiles at me in faint recognition of my repeated presence or of her youth perhaps unless women really did have more dignity then as if to say leave off, loneliness has its strength and beauty, like unrequited love. Have you ever stood he says once when we are still on terms for hours in the cold simply to catch a glimpse of someone? We are talking about a friend of his. The man must be sick he says I could never get that worked up. Perhaps you have never loved I say or maybe merely think perhaps he has never loved. Maybe I murmur no, I couldn't either. We are still on terms at that moment in time.

But as I let the street suck my blood while I still have blood to suck we are not on terms and a glimpse is better than no terms at all until I stand all drained of psychic energy from nothing not even a glimpse, glimpses being untimable in a live long day of a full irregular masculine timetable and walk away quickly as if none of it mattered to unnumb my limbs while I still have limbs to unnumb all the way to the small flat in the square block in the big lonely city.

But now there is no need. Nobody knows that my body lies there in my bed in the locked flat in the big city, its atoms all bombarded by those of the barbiturates and slowly undergoing the chemical reaction into compost that will feed no earth no worms no mulching vegetation, only the stinking air in the small room all windows closed. I die alone because I live alone. I give notice at work I have the telephone removed I stop the milk I tell the porter to forward my mail if any to Poste Restante where I call now and again, wearing the semblance of my temporal body, only to find there is no mail except the month's rent reminder and the quarter's demand for rates.

One day no doubt the rent man or the rate man or the gas man must come round and ring the bell and bang the door, and the disturbed molecules of wood will let the smell of my decay waft through and the police perhaps will scatter them with a battering ram or even with the mere brute force of uniformed bodies. I am well aware that I am acting out a fantasy since the porter has a passkey into the smell of my decay as into all our privacies.

It is because I am acting out a fantasy that I can wear the semblance of my temporal body and move about as if I existed, which of course I do. Anyone with enough love or hate exists even when out of mind or dead. Existence is not a temporal state but an energy which does not stop merely for lack of flesh although in many dead people this energy does degrade itself for lack of love so that it shrinks like a degenerate star into less than a pinpoint weighing many tons. Naturally they feel full of a heavy nothingness of which the rumour spreads apathetically sporadically through live matter like a transuranian element decaying over aeons into lead. And so this is what people in this needle of time think death is.

But I am acting out a fantasy of unrequited love or is it hate that has such driving force I can collect the semblance of my atoms and clothe myself in them and move about at will. I can also move about without the semblance of my atoms. I can do both because both exist in a potential choice which keeps me in a state of dither unable to decide which part of the fantasy I most want to act out: that of being invisibly present at my own death with all my friends aghast and shocked and sad or that of nobody knowing I have died. The first is stronger as a desire so strong it makes me take my life, suicide being a meaningless gesture which says I want to leave you today and come back tomorrow to see how you've taken it. The desire to be thus present at my own death is stronger than the desire that nobody should know I have died, but the fear in it is stronger still for I know the answer can only be a slight shock a shrug a sigh of relief. I have no friends and few acquaintances. So I move along two parallel lines of existence trying to have it both ways invisible most of the time and watching my few acquaintances, but also keeping up the pretence of appearing now and again at my usual haunts wearing the semblance of my temporal body so that nobody knows I have died. I fear their indifference more than I want their slight shock their guilt if any or their punishment.

Sooner or later however the choice will have to be made because in time the rent man or the rate man or the gas man will come round and use the passkey into the smell of my decay.

Unless of course I choose not to act out the fantasy. Then I would find annihilation and some sort of peace perhaps. My energy too would degrade itself for lack of love or hate into less than a pinpoint weighing many tons of heavy nothingness. That would be comforting.

But the driving force of the fantasy is irresistible. I do not really watch my few acquaintances or my no friends who do not hold me here but him and only him. Unlike the rent man or the rate man or the gas man he won't come knocking on my door ringing the bell scattering the molecules of wood with sheer brute force into the smell of my decay. Because we were not on terms.

And the being not on terms is the driving force of the fantasy. It drains me of atoms and even of their semblance so that I still stand in the last porch of the curved street and wait for a glimpse of him as he comes and goes. And the greater watching time afforded by my death spreads like a net which must by mere totality of coverage catch all the glimpses possible in the curved space of the street and more. Even the sights of the rich old lady have increased fivefold and for her smile I wear the semblance of my atoms now and again and hide behind the pillar in the double wisdom tooth at the end of the giant vampire's jaw. Watching him come and go.

The multiplying glimpses feed me with fresh particles of psychic energy so that although the vampire's jaw drains me of semblant atoms I in turn draw strength from the glimpses it provides with which I feed the hungry monster of my fantasy which grows and grows until I can be with him at all times and places. Without the fantasy I would cease to exist, fantasy being the existence which does not stop merely for lack of mass times the speed of light squared let alone for lack of the polynucleotides and complex proteins needed to activate a temporal body. Without the fantasy I would find some sort of peace perhaps.

He has another woman now reasonably since unable to accept the hurtful terms we were on I broke them a married one, a little less convenient as regards consideration not his strong point of her timetable as well as his but more convenient in her desires that don't extend to marriage. Not that she feels happy as a quick sly convenience. I am in a privileged position divested as I can be of my temporal atoms. He also rings her after the first time with clumsy gestures and finds her sad oh what a bore he says why take it like that not a whistling cavalier to shrug it off and move away as if that was what bothered her on the contrary that would be more welcome for shrug it off and move away is what he does in emotional effect if not in physical presence because complacently he equates physical presence with emotional effect no generosity of imagination or tenderness being required as well and my self-pity envelops her by analogy. He tells her the same things in the same words with the same performance. It's only way I can show you he says post-passionately as the nearest he can get to words of homage and she also doesn't say but thinks show me what, that even in this he is inconsiderate? So my angry self-pity envelops her by analogy but with an element of admiring envy at the way she makes more allowances. She knows and accepts as I in my real body know but do not accept that his emotions are low-powered, he has no reserves below the easy surface, his energy too would degrade itself quickly in death for lack of love into less than a pinpoint weighing innumerable tons of heavy nothingness, he would find peace he does. It is true that she is still in the gay light-hearted early phase I know so well and that in time his thoughtless words and manner will erode her gaiety. In time she must crumble from her light-hearted status as a quick sly convenience and bombard him with the atoms of a chain reaction, at which he will shrug be inar-ticulate move off exactly as he does when she accepts her status as a sly quick convenience. It makes no difference either way. Unless she is al-together more light-hearted through and through.

The rich old lady emerges out of the last house behind whose pillar I wear from invisibility-fatigue the semblance of my temporal body. She nods and smiles. Loneliness has its strength she says don't feed on him too long or you will lose the capacity for it. If it isn't too late she says will you come and take tea with me on Saturday? It would give me great pleasure to communicate with a young person. Madam if I am not alto-gether dead by then I should be delighted. Come come at your age I'll expect you at four.

He comes and goes. He walks along the double row of teeth in the curved jaw of the vampire. I do not reassume the invisibility which tires me out with vision and knowledge so that he sees me in my temporal body and crosses the road into the semi-circular gardens to avoid me reasonably enough or is it cowardly. In any case the force of the fantasy drives me to move my temporal body into his path for further punish-ment not only from his thoughtless words and manner but from the sudden change in me the moment we are on terms, a change to my early normal vision of an affable sluggish man, a static man nobody ever gets to know any better, who has revealed no hidden dynamism despite the benefit of the doubt given over and over and I look at his thick face and unregarding eyes and think I never would but know I did how could I? It is as if I had never known him, the last impression re-turning to the hello.

—Oh. Hello.

—How are you?

—Oh, all right. Terrible cold, though, don't come near me.

He sees my eroded gaiety and crumbling inconvenience and also thinks how could he but doesn't care whether he did or not.

—I wasn't going to. Nothing could be further from my mind.

—Oh I don't know. He laughs. I wouldn't say nothing. You look well.

Behind his words and manner there is nothing but his words and manner. Love is only the intense desire to know someone and becomes unrequited or is it hate when it finds no one there to know.

—Thank you for enquiring. The semblance of my atoms creates no semblance of communication. Even in death I say all the wrong things like why did you cross the road to avoid me, when I know the answer is my behaviour too embarrassing even for courtesy which never was his strong point.

—Me? I didn't . . . I always walk through the gardens. And things like are you happy? Now that we are on terms I endure fully the sudden change to my normal vision of a pleasant sluggish man with hardly an atom of love in all that flesh and hardly a pinpoint of interest or curiosity except the prying kind into the weaknesses of others that make him feel so good heavens, he says, I never ask myself such questions. What are you doing here?

—Walking suffering. I don't like suffering. It hurts.

—Oh? I'd got the impression you rather enjoyed it.

—So that was your reason. All the wrong things again but they get no reaction.

—Actually I'm on my way home. I went to town to do some shopping. Window-shopping I mean, I didn't find anything. I'm er—getting married.

—What!

—Thank you. Yes. Next week. I suppose, I couldn't prevail on you, if you would, I mean, if you're free, to give me away? As an old friend. I have no family. Saturday 11 o'clock at St. Martin's.

—Well I don't know. Let me see.

The pocket diary is blank for Saturday at 11 o'clock I know because he sees his quick convenience then and doesn't write it down. Besides in my parallel invisible state I can see Saturday and the wedding guests all made out of my psychic energy and its almost inexhaustible semblance of atoms. I even see the white carnation in his buttonhole. Thank you, how nice, I gather the idea tickles your fancy.

—Yes, well, it is rather amusing.

—And your wife, of course. I hope she'll come. Sorry it's so informal but I've only just thought of it. Asking you I mean.

—This is all very sudden. How did it, er, who's the lucky man? Are you sure not just rebounding?

—From the great love that was ours? Of course. So you see you owe me at least the gesture. How about you, have you found a new mistress?

—I don't want a mistress. If I did, no doubt I'd fix myself up with one.

—No doubt. Well, see you Saturday then. Collect me in the hall of my block at ten to, I'll have a hired car waiting. And please, no presents, we're going abroad immediately. Bye.

So the die is cast on keeping up the pretence that I am alive, appearing here and there in the semblance of my temporal body especially there on Saturday at 11 o'clock. Not that this way I avoid the answer to the fear inherent in the other course, the slight shock the shrug the sigh of relief if not at my death then at my removal and the resentment at even being asked for a last gesture. The parallel lines meet in the further punishment administered with his every word and manner but the driving force of the fantasy impels me along.

The matter of my rebound my present or future unhappiness and my wedding moves out of his mind as he walks towards his house, naturally since it has no existence except as the fantasy which does not stop for lack of flesh. But then the matter of his new mistress's happiness or otherwise does not dwell in his mind either. He never asks himself such questions. What do you see yourself as, I enquire in exasperation at his lack of enthusiasm for all things once when we are still on terms that drag my gaiety down into his conversational lethargy me, he says I don't see myself as anything I just drift. So that his image too must degrade itself in death for lack of love into less than a pinpoint weighing many tons of heavy nothingness which is what people in this needle of time think death is. And so it will be when I have ceased to act out the fantasy. A comforting thought. But the being not on terms is the driving force which impels me to invent new terms, for of course we are on terms even if only those of agreeing to give me away. The terms we are on feed the hungry monster of my fantasy which absorbs the hurts like immunising poison so that the early normal vision of an affable sluggish man dissolves and the dynamic image of his absence grows.

On the morning of my marriage he emerges from his house in the vampire's jaw alone and walks along the double row of giant teeth. His wife for reasons best known to herself namely that she has caught his germ or that he has dissuaded her declines to attend. His cancellation of the quick sly convenience fills me with joy and triumph at his small preference for a tickled fancy and in my invisibility I follow him. He has so few and such small preferences I can gloat over this one. There will be time enough to the church with the semblance of my no friends and few acquaintances. Nobody knows that my body lies in bed in my locked flat in the square block, rapidly undergoing the chemical reaction into compost that as yet feeds no earth, only the stinking air in the small room all windows closed. At the Poste Restante I collect a cheque for guineas from him.

The area of his street is residential, dead. So dead that a big hearse waits outside the last house in the crescent, heading two dark and empty cars. The boot is up, as if the coffin had just been slid in or a last bouquet or wreath of flowers added to the others and all the flowers are white.

He stops. Not out of superstition or to make a gesture of homage since gestures or words of homage do not come naturally to him if at all but because the white carnations remind him of his empty buttonhole. The area of his street is residential, dead, without a flower shop in sight.

He hesitates. I give him that, yes, I mark that up in his favour. It goes to join all the awkward short-lived tendernesses he uses when still uncertain of seduction, sham but tendernesses still and in his favour, weighing a little against the later hurts if not viewed in their light but in the light of the beginning when I so much want to count all in his favour. He looks at the house with the curtains drawn and the garlanded door half open. The coffin underneath the mass of white flowers waits for the few mourners about to emerge and the murmuring undertaker.

The hesitation is over. His left hand quickly picks a white carnation from the end wreath on the hearse, his right hand joins the left to fix it in his buttonhole as he walks quickly on.

The rich old lady lies inside the coffin and smiles, turning her dead face towards me all surrounded with thin white hair. Death has its strength and I don't mind she says. I have seen life and willingly give a flower of my death to adorn a married man about to give away his young escaped mistress into the hands of death.

I mind, however.

—My dear child, why?

—Because I created the flower for his buttonhole out of my atoms, allowing only for the semblance of a result, not for a real result with a real origin and in you of all people.

—And the origin with a free will gesture in another human being, in two other human beings instead of in your fantasy shocks you?

—Dear child, don't mind so much. Come come at your age I'll see you at four.

The real result with a real origin galvanises me into the semblance of my atoms all in white down the stairs into the hall just as he enters. He looks astonished, white? he says. The porter looks even more astonished at my presence which waves gaily sails through the door and folds itself into the hired car, followed by all those molecules of thick flesh with hardly an atom of love beneath the white carnation.

—I thought it was informal.

—It is. But one only dies once.

—Oh come.

—I'm glad you thought of a buttonhole. And thank you for the cheque. You shouldn't have.

—You look very fetching he says with surprise regret boredom impatience I feel too disembodied to care. It is the first compliment he has ever paid me apart from the privilege of being seduced by him with awkward short-lived sham tendernesses the only way he can show me what?

The church is fuller than I expected. All my no friends and more than my few acquaintances are there made out of more than my psychic energy on both sides of the aisle. I do not know the wedding guests on the bridegroom's side. I know the bridegroom a little, the skilful tendernesses he uses for seduction still weighing against the brutal annihilation to come when he destroys the fantasy and its energy degenerates for lack of love into less than a pinpoint of heavy nothingness. I walk the aisle on my once lover's arm to Parcell's Trumpet Voluntary. I promise to obey. I have no choice. Because one day the rent man or the rate man or the gas man will come round and ring the bell or bang the door and the disturbed molecules of wood will let the smell of my decay waft through. But I shall not be present at my own death my friends aghast and shocked and sad for the answer is a shrug a sigh of relief at my removal and my non-existence with the energy of my fantasy degenerated to one pinpoint of heavy nothingness. That will be comforting but you must kiss the bride yes kiss the bride.

I don't know who the best man is who kisses me. A friend of the bridegroom his façade perhaps, the skilful tendernesses he uses for seduction until the fantasy becomes destroyed. You too must kiss the bride.

He hesitates. I give him that, yes, I mark that up in his favour he has given me away made his last gesture paid his five guineas that is enough. I turn my face towards him in its veil of tulle and see him start with horror.

So the process has begun already. The fantasy loses its driving force and cannot hold the semblance of my atoms in a pretence of life. What does he see? The dead face of the rich old lady he robbed whose white carnation he stole to adorn the tickled fancy of a married man giving away his young escaped mistress into the hands of death? Or is it my dead face he sees, its atoms all bombarded by those of the barbiturates, rapidly undergoing the chemical change to compost that as yet feeds no earth no worms no mulching vegetation, only the stinking air in the small room all windows closed?

He draws away. The semblances of the chief wedding guests who are witnesses in the vestry laugh and tease him as we drink champagne a little out of place for there is no reception. I have arranged it so. No you can't get out of it you gave her away you must propose the toast you too must kiss the bride. I turn my face towards him in its veil of tulle and see him stare in horror. I search for my reflection in his eyes, each one of which throws back a dead face, in the left eye very old with thin white hair and a deep regarding look, in the right eye young but crumbling with eroded gaiety, skeletal, the mouth curved like a vampire's jaw and the skull surrounded in white tulle he yells.

—All right, keep your precious carnation!

He flings it in my decomposing face. A grey aisle of silence forms through the wedding guests as he bolts along it to the vestry door into the church where the remaining guests wait for the triumphal march and down the aisle of the church into the world of nice casual emotions and familiar residential streets that stand secure in parallels except for one that curves like the jaw of a giant vampire with a double row of teeth which in my day has sucked my blood.

In a month of time no doubt the gas man or the rent man will ring the bell bang on my door and smell the smell of my decay as it wafts through the disturbed molecules of wood. Or the police perhaps will scatter them with a battering ram even with the brute force of uniformed bodies unless the porter uses his passkey into the privacy of my death.

The fantasy has lost its driving force and cannot hold the semblance of my atoms in a pretence of life. My no friends and my few acquaintances dissolve, the bridegroom takes the energy of my pretence and in less than no time degrades it for lack of love into less than an anti-atom of heavy nothingness. I have a teatime date with the rich old lady at four. The process of degeneration is painful but comforting as far as I remember I have a teatime date with understanding as far as I can tell the process is painful but comforting as far as I

Troglodyte

My friends were a little dubious when I announced my decision to
become a troglodyte. But after all, I had made the decision partly
in order to get away from the dubiousness of my friends. I should have
spared them their dubiousness, I suppose, by not telling them. On the
other hand, it is the telling that strengthens a decision from a vague
idea to an obligation and from an obligation to an accomplished fact.

So here I am in my cave, which is, as Cortado said, cool in summer,
warm in winter. Cortado was not dubious at all, and from the first,
aimed to raise the eventual rent of his cave by pretending hard to sell
me something I didn't want. Wouldn't I prefer to rent a *casa* on the hills
behind the city, viewing the island's central mountains on one side, and
on the other the distant sea? His pricing eye cash-registered my shapeless dress of glazed cotton, then my shabby suitcase. Something *más
económico* perhaps, a very small *casa*? But he knew quite well that I was
serious in my foreign eccentricity, and I knew quite well that he
couldn't really put me in the way of renting a villa, any more than I rent
one. All the same, he behaved like an estate agent to the end.

'Cool in summer, warm in winter,' Cortado said. 'And this cave is
among the best in the village, as you can see, it's not every cave that has
its own private staircase.'

This is true, in a way. The steps, gleaming white-washed in the sun,
climb over the roof of the cave below, which juts out like a porch, a
squashed sort of porch on account of the steps climbing up one side.
But the steps are only there because Cortado's cave happens to be the
first of a row to which some access had to be made from the lower row.
Cortado's cave, like the others in the row, is set back a little, so that a
ridge of flat rock winds along in front of the caves and above the

porches underneath. This ridge is bordered with a parapet full of geraniums, forming a kind of long balcony for all his neighbours to the left and of course for his own front door. My front door, now.

I haven't yet found out whether Cortado pays rent for his cave. The other troglodytes are very reticent on the subject, unwilling to help me work out just what Cortado's profit might be. Presumably anyone originally able to build a front wall and door to any one of these caves thereby established a right to it, but the village as it has now stood for generations may well have evolved a system of sales and transferences and nominal rents to someone or other. I only know that Cortado was fairly zealous to let me have it, and found somewhere else to sleep with remarkable ease.

'The Guanches made the caves,' he said to me on his first courtesy call after I had moved in. I nodded as I handed him a thimble cup of syrupy black coffee. I knew the history of the islands and had seen many of the caves, some as abandoned small black holes distantly high up a mountain face that looked from afar like a disease, some more accessible as developed villages, gay and painted and alive. This one was fairly high up, and the path below ours edged a mere three feet wide between the caves and a sheer drop.

'They made the caves to hide from us Spaniards.'

He caught my look of mock surprise, melting it into amusement. For despite the visibly more recent African blood in his veins, he had first proudly told me that he himself was a Guanche, embroidering a little too fast about his family owning the cave for generations and being descended from Princess Guayarmina herself. His black pupils glittered in the sun that flecked his face through the battered brim of an old straw hat as he sat on the penultimate step, sipping his coffee. He refused to come inside now that I was his tenant. The glitter in his eyes dismissed his earlier boast as salesmanship.

'*Café solo* is bitter,' he said, so simply and with such a distant look towards the mountains that it did not seem at all rude, or in any way connected with the coffee he was drinking. 'It tastes nicer with a little milk, but still strong. We call it *café cortado*.' Still watching the mountains, he grinned with pleasure at this elaborate joke, which he must have told many times, since it was the explanation of his nickname. But his eyeballs had moved imperceptibly in my direction at the climax, and his pleasure was partly derived from my appreciative smile.

He got up suddenly, placed the tiny cup on the parapet, bowed and said with careful politeness: '*Señorita* should not be *sola* either. *Adios, Señorita*, and thank you.'

He went slowly down the steps, turned back at the bottom and raised his hand in farewell, almost but not quite to the brim of his old straw hat. Then he walked on along the narrow path below without looking back and vanished round the corner of the mountain.

Some of the other caves, I have discovered, go deeper, with a second and sometimes a third room at the back. But Cortado's is a bachelor flat.

It is sumptuously furnished, for a cave, I mean. There is a wooden table that wobbles on the uneven floor, a stool and a huge old bergère with its insides strewing a bit. A shelf with hooks for coathangers has been nailed or screwed into the rock and a cretonne curtain hangs over it. There is a brazier for cooking and a marble-topped washstand with china jug, basin and soap-dish in matching roses and lilies, and a china slop-pail from another set with cherubs and ribbons. The chamberpot has marguerites. There is also a grandfather clock that chimes, and finally a brass double bed with a mattress of stuffing, not straw, some blankets for the chilly nights and a pair of sheets. I do my own laundry, that is, I manage my personal things in the stream further down the mountain on the communal wash-day, but Maria Nieves, who lives below me, does the sheets for me. She spreads them on the rocks with a stone at each corner and they dry on the same day, bleaching in the sun.

Like my neighbours, I am living almost entirely on *gofio*, the toasted maize flour which is mostly eaten as a kind of porridge, but can also be mixed in soup or spread on bread or used as flour for frying, when there is anything to fry—pimentoes, chiefly. So I am getting fat. The sea is too far to go swimming, and although I do my small shopping and other chores, I can only walk for exercise in the cool of the evening.

And then I prefer to sit, for that is when everyone else sits, just outside their front door, in twos and threes, gossiping, and one doesn't want to singularise oneself. So I sit outside my door, receiving, or I sit outside someone else's door, visiting.

During the day I sit inside my cave, in the broken bergère, gazing at the hole of bright light and meditate. The troglodytes are not in the least dubious about this.

'The *señorita* is meditating,' they shout down the path if children are making a lot of noise or anyone officious-looking is on the way to disturb me. I meditate to the noise of Maria's radio from below. Maria's radio is permanently on, and Maria would, I feel sure, feel naked in her waking hours without its enveloping noise. And soon I too learn to dress into it and to undress out of it, and to sit in my clothing of noise, staring at the hole of bright light outside my cave.

Through the hole of bright light I can see, beyond the geraniums on my parapet, another wall of caves, sideways, to the right, and to the left a more distant ridge over other caves, topped by a cluster of young palm trees, blowing sometimes in the breeze like shingled heads; and beyond all that the sky and the slope of an orange mountain. It is astonishing how hypnotic a hole of bright light and colour can be when stared at from a darkness, for of course, although the walls of my cave are whitewashed in pale pink, they seem quite dark compared to the hole of bright light. Sometimes I have visions. I only mention them in passing since I am not sure which kind they are.

'The *señorita* should not be *sola*,' Cortado said for the sixteenth time when he came to collect the rent for the sixteenth time, today.

'But I like being alone, Cortada.'

'You spend much time with Maria Nieves, don't you?'

'She is a kind person.'

'You like her cave better, perhaps?'

'No, no. Of course not.'

'It is bigger. But then she has a large family.'

'Naturally.'

'She has, too, a radio.'

'Indeed she has.'

'But Cortado,' I added after a pause, 'I don't want a radio here. I assure you, I am quite, quite satisfied with looking at the sky. I have visions sometimes,' I said shyly.

That was two days ago. This afternoon two men struggled up the narrow paths with a large cardboard box on a porter's push-trolley. All the troglodytes came out to watch and cheer their efforts, and I went out too, cheering with them. But when I saw that everyone was giving excited directions, pointing at me, my heart sank. Cortado was nowhere to be seen.

The push-trolley reached my steps at last. The two men lifted the big box off the trolley and carried it up. Carefully they deposited the box on the floor of my little forecourt and started to cut the string.

'What is it? If it's a radio, I don't want it.'

They shook their heads and said together, shouting above the nasal sobs from Maria's radio: '*Momento señora, momentito.*'

I waited.

I nearly screamed when I saw the two antennae of the portable aerial. The two men grinned at my childish excitement.

It was not until the familiar dead window peered out of the packing straw that my voice found the right frequency again.

'Take it away,' I said calmly but loudly above the lament of Maria's radio. 'I don't want a television set. No television.'

'Where is the electric plug?' one man asked above the strumming from Maria's radio.

There was a long silence, that is to say, there was only the strumming from Maria's radio. The strumming broke into a wail.

The troglodytes were crowded on the row up the steps, and behind me on the parapet.

'Cortado said there was electricity.'

'Not in this cave,' I said, triumphantly, above the lament from Maria's radio. 'Oil lamp. See?'

'But the radio?'

'Cortado said it could run from the same plug.'

They were shouting both together, above the twanging from Maria's radio, and pointing down at the sound as if it proved something. 'We brought a two-way adapter and a very long flex. Here, you see. Over the parapet.'

'Maria's radio,' I said as the song whirled to a stop, 'is a battery radio.'

Everyone started talking at once, drowning the announcer on Maria's radio.

'Some of the caves have electricity.'

'Yes, but only down below.'

'It's not far.'

'A hundred metres.'

'Fifty.'

'You could have it down there and visit it.'

'Maria nearly had the electricity brought up.'

'That was last year.'

'I always said—'

'Then we could all see it.'

Cortado came this morning to stare morosely at the unborn television set which is standing on the marble washstand. The jug and basin had been removed to a dark corner of the cave floor, and when I need them I place them on the wooden table.

'I thought, I rent, you enjoy the pictures, you pay me higher rent. The *señorita* should not be *sola*.'

I was touched. But firm.

'I am not alone, Cortado. My cave has been crowded with visitors all day. Even without pictures, the set fascinates them.' I added gently: 'You will have to take it away, Cortado.' He looked pained. 'You see, I prefer to look at your beautiful sky. It makes much prettier pictures.'

'Yes, the sky is fine. But you should not be alone.'

It was then that he gave me his dark look. Until that moment I had not at all understood what he was getting at.

'Cortado, you are not a marriage agent.' I put it nicely to save his sensibility. 'I enjoy being alone. And besides, I know what I look like.'

That was my first mistake. I will not pretend that I do not feel sensitive about being so patently an English old maid. It was precisely to avoid those hunters for free sex among frustrated female tourists that I came here, away from even the cheapest of hotels. But one should never draw attention to one's own defects.

A string of compliments followed.

I was disappointed with Cortado. I had not expected that of him.

'Who, in any case,' I asked, as ever clumsy with compliments, on account of trying so hard to remember that they are false, 'who would want to keep me company?'

That was my second mistake.

'There are *señores*,' he said with a flourish of his brown hand.

The jug and basin are back on the marble washstand. The unborn television set now sits on the floor near the table, like a stool, although nobody would dare to use it as such. For it is much revered by most of my visiting neighbours, who have all heard of television and are convinced that it works for me alone. They tend to sit hypnotised in front of it, hoping that they too will be vouchsafed a vision, and perhaps believing that they have been. Little Dolores, Maria's second eldest aged eleven, seems to think it is a new kind of magic mirror in which I can see her future when she sits before it. Old Paquita Jimenez, who tells fortunes, is quite annoyed.

Maria had advised me to keep all this popularity of mine from Cortado, who prefers me to be *sola*, so that he can go on trying to persuade me not to be. On the whole, however, they come in the evenings, when their work is done, and leave me to myself by day. They respect my solitude as a visionary.

Cortado does not respect my solitude, at least, not as a visionary. I shouldn't, perhaps, have told him about my visions, for he has become more and more dubious. This morning he came like a destructive angel.

'I have a friend.'

'I am glad.'

'My friend is an electrician. In the capital.'

'Cortado, please don't insist.'

'He can bring the electricity up from the lower caves. For me he will charge nothing. The cable he will steal from his shop.'

'I cannot receive pictures through a stolen cable.'

'Well the *señorita* may pay for the cable if she wishes.'

Winter has come, and the hole of bright light is less bright. I have had to borrow extra blankets.

'It *could* be warm in winter!' Cortado darkly altered the tense when I queried his original promise.

The pressure of these hints continues. Either Or, Cortado seems to be saying.

So here I am in my cave, or rather, in Cortado's cave, he has moved back in. Spring has come and it is so hot that Cortado just sits in the broken bergère with his feet on the cardboard box full of straw that once packed the unborn television set. As he sits, he draws a small income from the television set, which has now been born at last, down in one of the bottom caves, the big one which is the troglodyte village shop, and the shop makes small profit from allowing people in to watch at ten centimos an evening. Even Cortado goes down, and I feel a little lonely, deserted by all my friends. But by day he just sits, with his feet on a cushion on the cardboard box full of straw, and from the cool depth of rock he gazes at the hole of bright light and the orange mountain, to the noise of Maria's radio. He says he is meditating. He hardly moves except to remove the cushion and use the cardboard box as a private table when I serve his meals.

I eat at the wobbly table. I cook the *gofio* and do the small shopping and mend his socks and wash our clothes in the stream further down the mountain on the communal washday. I have learnt how to beat the sheets clean because I can't afford to pay Maria Nieves any more. They dry on the same day, bleaching in the sun, now that the winter drizzles are over. I also pay Cortado his rent on which we live. I don't have visions any more, so it doesn't matter where they came from.

It was lovely being a troglodyte, but I am beginning to feel a little dubious about it. Perhaps I shall go back to London soon. Before the winter sets in, anyway. Or after the winter, before it gets too warm again.

The Foot

The victim to be haunted is female. And beautiful. This makes a difference. She has the habit of confidence, but also a greater adjustment to achieve. In the intact body there is a constant stream of impulses bombarding the cortex from the nerve-ends in the muscles, which bombardment is evenly balanced on both sides. But when the body is no longer intact a neuro-muscular imbalance results which throws additional strain on the sensitised cerebrum and upsets the previous state of equilibrium. It is difficult to estimate at this relatively early stage how far her habit of confidence will counter the despair at the adjustment to be achieved and therefore weaken the imbalance in the stream of impulses reaching the cortical areas.

The victim is female and very beautiful, as far as can be judged at present with her eyes closed peacefully in analgesic slumber unaware of pain. It is easy to forget the full extent of beauty when the eyes are shut and the neuroblasts asleep to agony. Eyes open can bring beauty alive with awareness of pain terror despair or anger, not to mention desire and liquid tenderness or even the alluring invitation down the pathways to the womb the tomb the cavern the ebb and flow of time linked to the sun-devouring moon the monster chasm of death and timelessness that draws man like a magnet from the moment he is conscious of a fall a wrench of umbilical tissue rough manhandling tumbling lying in soft cloud sucking at heaven severed weight of body on stumbling legs and fall, fall through the days and minutes. Eyes open can bring archetypes alive but now they are closed on a white ashen face sheathed in pale lanky hair like dead nerve fibres that conduct no pain along pale lanky limbs except for the right leg amputated above the knee. Pity. A thousand pities bombard the cortex from the nerve-ends in the stump-neuroma where the axons proliferate excitedly and send back false messages of pain that find at present no decoder in the slumbering central image of a limb no longer there. We have however no room for pity in the haunting game.

It is a proven scientific fact that women have a higher pain threshold than men. Which makes the task more difficult but interesting. Men are no challenge. Yet even within this distinction the threshold varies from subject to subject and from time to time for there is rhythm in the haunting game as in any other according to stress fatigue drugs general constitution previous equilibrium distraction violent activity including sex and the psychiatrist recommends electroencephalic treatment despite statistics proudly quoted out of nineteen cases eight improved six relapsed after improvement three unchanged two worse as if that proved anything and some are unduly sensitive he says in his report. In every case the treatment improved the patient's attitude towards the pain so that he or she was less distressed by it. True, and annoying. But there are ways to recreate distress. Often the treatment altered the nature of the pain he proudly adds and thus in several amputees the position of the phantom limb and its concomitant pain were altered rather than relieved. Yes, there are ways.

Still, they do make the task more and more difficult. In the old days they believed merely in conditioning methods, an empty name for the attempt to raise the threshold simply through the refusal of those in authority to admit the existence of the phantom pain. As if one could refuse to admit the existence of a ghost. They have to admit it now. Unfortunately they also study it, which does make the task more difficult, even though they do not wholly understand it yet. Why, for instance, the ghost pain haunts at such an unpredictable rhythm, leaving an amputee in peace for twenty years and suddenly appearing, inexorable, excruciating. Or why it materialises in the phantom shape of the foot only, or the hand, not the whole limb, although the limb is also a phantom and the real pain in the stump aches in every neurone. And yet it is obvious that to be effective pain must attack the most active therefore vulnerable part of the central memory-image, the extremities once in touch with earth air and water, the soles that bear the whole weight of existence as man transmutes his structural archetypes from curled to lying to upright position and learns the shapes of time food light dark play by lingering breasts limbs balls cuddly animals. But there are other reasons. Ghosts must preserve some mystery.

If they can. Certainly knowledge is advancing. White sun, for instance, or audio-analgesia to be more precise can annihilate us if only for a while. But leucotomy is the great enemy, resorted to quite openly in cases of intractable phantom pain. Nice word, intractable, in view of the way we phantoms infiltrate ourselves down the pathways of pain, down the spinothalamic tract to be precise, not that I'm partial to words, they can be enemies too, but I like words that bring alive my task my journey down the pathways of pain, down the spinothalamic tract into which they now however introduce electrodes in a stereotactic procedure to produce a phantom pain and out where exactly to coagulate. Very dangerous. Obviously, since the phantom is not the real one but electrically raised. The result is only too often spasticism in the other limb on the same side and loss of upward conjugate gaze. Eyes open can bring beauty alive with awareness terror pain despair or anger not to mention the alluring invitation down the pathways to the womb and all the rest. A thirty-year-old woman not as attractive but still desirable and successfully haunted by an excruciating phantom in the foot no longer there was very agitated and importunate says Mr. Poole the surgeon but after a leucotomy she became calm, the importunacy vanished and she only referred to the pain when asked if it existed. It is true he innocently proudly adds that she then said it was excruciating. Ghosts must preserve some power.

If they can. There are still ways of lowering the threshold. Severe mental deprivation or retardation for example raise it and the highly intelligent undoubtedly suffer more than the plethoric unimaginative like the last one a man plethoric unimaginative. That was a hopeless attempt. It's best to haunt the intelligent. They are not used to responding fully with their bodies and the shock is greater.

But it also makes the task more difficult in other ways, though interesting. The present victim is not only beautiful, pale of course, ashen pale in all that hair ashen pale from lack of violent activity including sex but intelligent. She thinks about me, thus creating my shape, together with its pain, thus giving me existence as a foot, the prettiest foot I have ever been and perhaps was before the leg was lacerated wrenched and crushed in all that twisted car metal because it's hard to tell whether I once was her real foot or not, so completely do I now achieve identification as her phantom foot slim long and gracefully arched and well sprung above a most shapely big toe. That's where I manage to hurt most. But she thinks intelligently about me, in the full knowledge that I am not really there attached to the long space that is her phantom leg also not there. She winds me round with other thoughts like boring details of hospital routine that loom larger than life or intrinsic worth and wrap each phantom fibre of me like a medullary sheath at times. But at times only for I have my rhythm and several other amputees to haunt which would tend to prove that I never was her personal real foot in a full schedule with necessary rest-periods to withdraw my atoms in quiescence before gathering them up into the neuroblasts that will create me anew within her brain along the spinothalamic tract and the efferent fibres down to the neuroma in the stump where the axons of the severed nerves proliferate wildly and send back false messages to the cortical areas that will soon when the strong tranquilliser dies build up from them the central image of a limb no longer there but wrenched and lacerated crushed and cut now cleanly, surgically away, if cleanly it can be called with such a tumorous antheap in the stump. And now she thinks about me, giving me strength, existence, and creating my shape, her slim long phantom foot, her unendurable phantom pain.

She cries quietly. I find this very exciting. The imitation neurones I am now composed of agitate their dendrites like tremulous antennae interlacing intermingling or the frictioning legs of flies that swarm as the cell bodies dance through the synapses and I want her to scream.

But she cries quietly. She is not only beautiful but brave, pale of course ashen pale in all that ashen hair like dead nerve fibres that conduct no pain themselves but sheathe the white face crisped in a cramp agony of sharp nails driven into the bones of the metatarsus and the ball of the foot that only exists within the white matter of the mid-brain as greyish white as her face and as crisped in its creation of my shape with its concomitant pain, dear?

—Yes, nurse. It's very bad. But give me another injection. I must learn to deal with it.

Not if I can help it.

—That's right, dear. I wasn't going to. It's time for your percussion soon.

—Oh no.

—Oh yes. You know it'll do you good.

—But it's agony. And it doesn't help at all.

Alas it does, it is the death of me, although it hurts her real pain in the stump neuroma.

—It's agony at first, love. Like wearing the padded cast the day after the operation. But then the pressure gradually deadened the pain, didn't it? It's the same with percussion. You'll see, in time. Like tapping a bad tooth.

—Temporarily perhaps. But it doesn't cure the tooth does it. And the tooth exists, and is sick. Why should banging my stump with a mallet stop the pain in a foot I merely imagine?

Her intelligence will be the death of me, despite the lower threshold it creates to help me.

—And why do I get pain in the imagined foot anyway, and not in the whole leg? I imagine the leg too. And the stump hurts like hell. But that's different, it's real pain, so it's bearable, however acute.

—Yes dear, I know.

—Do you, nurse? Pain is so personal.

—Subjectiva dear, that's right. You'll be coming on nicely once you recognise that.

—My foot is an object. Outside myself. It exists.

—In your mind, love. Only in your mind. Mr. Poole explained it to you, didn't he?

—Oh yes, I know. The central nervous system can't get rid of its body-image, it's got so used to it after all those years. Twenty-two years to be precise. As if that helped. Only twenty-two. Why did I have to go with Denis in his crazy car? I didn't even like him. It's so unfair, it's—

—Now my dear, don't upset yourself. You'll only make it worse.

—It hurts, it hurts, I can't bear it, nurse, please give me something, I can't bear it.

She cries much more than quietly now, she shouts, she sobs, she yells, she gasps. I find it very exciting. The imitation neurones I am composed of agitate their dendrites like mad ganglia that arborise the system as the cell bodies dance along the axis cylinder within the fibres of the foot that isn't there, move backwards now, tugging away from the interlaced antennae as if trying to wrench themselves from some submicroscopic umbilical tie anchored into soft tissue, caught into bone, straining, straining to freedom birth and terror of time and space as the impulses race down the fibrils and create me, shape me and I ache strongly, I swell to huge existence that possesses her wholly and loves her loves her loves and hurts her unendurably until the cortical area can only respond by switching off the supply of blood along the nerves going out of the spinal cord so that she faints.

She looks so beautiful, so white and ashen pale in all that ashen hair like dead nerve fibres that conduct no pain themselves but sheath the white face peaceful now with conjugate upward gaze vanished beyond the slit eyelids to face the darker phantoms of the womb the tomb the cavern the ebb and flow of endless tides linked to the sun-devouring moon monster of chasm death and timelessness that draws the human soul like a magnet from the moment of the first fall wrench of umbilical muscle rough manhandling tumbling lying in soft cloud sucking at heaven severed from weight of body on stumbling legs and fall through days and minutes. Eyes open can bring archetypes alive and love that draws me to her like a magnet as she wakes and there there, love, lie quietly you'll feel better now.

—Yes. Thank you nurse.

As if she had done anything.

—Nurse.

—Yes, love?

—Is it true that children amputated before the age of four don't get phantom pains? Mr. Poole told me.

They do like to remind us of our powerless spheres. I feel exhausted, impotent.

—Well, if Mr. Poole told you, it must be true, mustn't it?

—That doesn't follow. Mr. Poole says a lot of things to patients to cheer them up. But like all doctors he's so busy he forgets we're individuals. For instance the other day, during percussion, he said—

—That reminds me, it's time. Are you all right now dear?

She retreats as usual into her obsession with Mr. Poole the surgeon the knife-man the castrator. She drowns in Mr. Poole, dipping her nerve-ends in soft surrounding tissue as in watery oedema, wrapping each phantom fibre of me with a medullary sheath of myelin that winds me round with thoughts of Mr. Poole and all that Mr. Poole has said in molecular detail to relieve soothe stimulate and occupy. I do not mind however at present being thus wound round cut off castrated as a phantom limb for I have temporarily spent my energy in possessing her so hugely hurtfully and I must rest recuperate my atoms while the rubber mallet knocks at her stump neuroma for ten minutes of time until with each knock several hundred unmyelinated nerve-fibres degenerate and after days weeks months curl up and die. But the real pain in her stump does not concern me, being as she so wisely says real therefore bearable. I merely take advantage of its existence in the early stages to increase my shape my hugeness my hold on her, I borrow its pain returning it with impulse interest. I draw my main strength though from the central image of me, so that after months of intimate relationship I am able to create myself out of this central image without recourse to the pain in the stump which may have vanished almost entirely after years or recur just intermittently according to stress and strain but unrelatedly to my sudden visitations. Ghosts have their own rhythms, must preserve independence, mystery.

I am beginning to miss her. It's always a bad sign when I start analysing my methods of self-creation self-absorption more like. She is herself absorbed away from me in Mr. Poole, who is gentlemanly with silvering hair and sexy eyes he knows just how to use to arouse the right degree of emotional involvement in his patients. He comes into the women's ward saying why haven't you brushed that lovely hair young lady and where's your handbag sweetie there take out your compact and a little lipstick too I like my patients to look feminine even the day after there that's better I thought you were so pretty on the operation table but a little pale as if anyone could look pretty in an oxygen mask. Even the men respond from submerged rivalry for his good looks frustration father-dependence and castration fears well founded as he taps their stumps with a rubber mallet in percussion therapy talking softly of problems pains and phantoms and get quite annoyed when Dr. Willett does it instead.

When is she coming back? Is it ten minutes or ten days since I last possessed her? I am losing track of time, always a ghostly failing when out of sense out of mind. She doesn't think of me. She is absorbed in Mr. Poole's silvering hair sexy eyes and soft words like young lady very pleased with you which flow even through the neurilemma across the myelin sheaths of every fibre and send impulses down the unsolid structures of the fibrils past the nodes where somehow they transmute into unformulated other words my little girl my love my sweet good little girl that float their chaotic particles around the entire autonomous system back up the spine into the thalamus with no more than a mild thermal sensation in the phantom foot as I grow jealous at a distance in lost space and time. I should have gone with her. But he would have observed me. And I was tired. And now I am restless at her absence from me.

He is explaining to her in a suave and sexy voice that the phantom pain is related to a central excitatory state with emphasis on the internuncial pool of the spinal cord or in other words my dear the higher sensory centres, with resulting summation of abnormal stimuli and a persistence of the pain pattern due to higher-level involvement. What is summation she asks to hide her confusion at the word involvement.

I'm sorry darling oh he calls everyone darling it's his therapeutic way you're so intelligent I forget you're not professional that too is his therapeutic way with her it merely means the total sum, you know, all the abnormal stimuli working together at once. And internuncial well you've heard of a nuncio haven't you, a messenger or ambassador of the Pope, it's the same with the nerves, they send messengers who gather together in the internuncial pool, like a typing pool you know, that's why I'm called Poole, ha, I receive all the nerve messages of all my patients and I sort them out and soothe them, like the pool of Lethe darling, so that they don't hurt any more, you see. For a while at least. Until your next visit.

—You seem intent on building up an emotional dependence in me. If you go on like that I'll get the phantom pain every time I'm due to see you.

—Now don't be too intelligent, sweetie, or you'll make it worse.

—Why abnormal stimuli working all together? What's abnormal about me?

—Not you, darling. You're a normal healthy lovely girl and you will soon be leading a normal healthy lovely life if you're good and do as I say.

The words flow through the myelin sheaths of every nerve and send impulses up and down the unsolid structures of the fibrils past the nodes where somehow they transmute to a normal healthy love life not quite formulated as they float in scattered particles slowly around the autonomous system back into the cerebrospinal and drown in the inter-nuncial pool before reaching the thalamus. She lies calm serene almost euphoric on her bed her open eyes alive with liquid tenderness and the alluring invitation down the pathways to the womb the ebb and flow of time linked to the sun-devouring moon white chasm of heaven and timelessness that draws me like a magnet from the moment I am conscious of my rebirth in desire to recreate my shape her phantom foot and devastate her beauty with my aching hugeness as an intractable phantom pain.

She shall love me want me need me despite her intelligence or even because of. She shall desire me to recreate my shape her phantom foot in her mind for the soft-voiced sexy-eyed attention of Mr. Poole the knife-man the castrator of that shape once in intimate touch with earth air water mother belly and bearing the whole weight of her existence in upright position on that shape of bone flesh fibre skin deeply engraved within the cellular composition of the left mid-brain at the level of the superior colliculus six millimetres lateral to the aqueduct of Sylvius in the region of the pain pathways. She shall cherish her symptoms.

How strong I was on that first day when she came to from dreamless anaesthetic nothingness and wanted to get up convinced her leg her foot were there after all the surgeon having somehow mended soothed plasticised remade the crushed and lacerated limb that now just dully ached through the still slumbering nerves. I watched her wake, so beautiful in her pallor sheathed with pale gold like myelin round dead fibres that conduct no pain. And the astonishment hope wonder in her sleepy siren's eyes that seemed to surface from deep waters moving with the sun-devouring moon great chasm of death and timelessness to which man must return drawn like a magnet from the moment of the fall the wrench of umbilical placenta rough manhandling tumbling lying in soft tissue sucking at the day that streams its minutes into weening separation weight of body on crumbling legs and fall through months and years. Even then I knew in a split atom of time bombarded by her beauty that it would have to be the higher-level involvement for my pains and I felt awed but strong with resulting summation of abnormal stimuli my shape quite hypertrophied though slim still in her mind and gracefully arched the prettiest foot I have ever been and perhaps was before her leg was lacerated crushed in all that twisted car metal.

The optic thalamus in the cerebral cortex was working hard and suddenly awake she saw me clear as I stretched my imitation metatarsus long gracefully arched towards the malleolar prominences on either side of her slim ankle up the shapely shin the rounded knee the dimple in the flesh of the popliteal fossa behind the knee till suddenly she threw back the bedclothes saw the stump bandaged into gaping void and gasped, then started moaning like an animal or a woman about to come. It was very exciting. But annihilating. I had existed so strong so hypertrophied and so sensuously detailed till she saw with her own eyes that I wasn't there and I almost ceased to be. But her terror her suffering as she panted galvanised my impulses into the free nerve-terminations of her pain fibres afferent proprioceptive and she screamed, oh joy ineffable. I knew then that the visioerotic element of her inner eye would always help me despite her intelligence or perhaps because of.

Words are my enemies. The words of Mr. Poole and Dr. Willett but especially Mr. Poole soft-voiced and sexy-eyed with his demands for lipstick hairbrushing self-confidence vanity and his explanations that soothe strengthen her understanding. She winds me round with words that formulate new thoughts of her mother her boyfriends and her job past present future which wrap each fibre of me like a medullary sheath at times. But only at times for I have my rhythm and although too engrossed obsessed too highly involved now with her to haunt other amputees I need my rest-periods. Not too long however. I am beginning to need her more than my rest-periods, to ache for her recognition of my existence, of my shape as a foot that belongs to her ineradicably and intimately within her cerebrospinal system bombarding it through all its impulse-bearing tracts with an intractable pain. The real danger of words is that they create thoughts which lead to other thoughts and these if stimulating and distracting and absorbing enough may smother me altogether or knock me out like a percussion mallet until my imitation unmyelated nerve-fibres degenerate curl up and die. If she starts thinking constructively about her future for instance. But there are ways. The words of Mr. Poole do have a side-effect that helps me, building up as she so intelligently said an emotional dependence from visit to visit the intelligent recognition which can in no wise prevent. For his soft-voiced and sexy-eyed attention she too often desires to recreate my phantom shape her foot once in intimate touch with earth air water mother belly and bearing the whole weight of her existence in upright position on that structure of bone flesh fibre skin now pierced with sharp nails driven into the metatarsus and the ball of the foot that only exists as an image deeply engraved within the left midbrain as greyish white as her face and as crisped in its creation of my shape she cherishes with its concomitant phantom pain.

—You are cherishing your symptoms my dear says Mr. Poole severely with a nevertheless gentle tap on the stump the neuroma almost circumscribed mature now non-proliferating healed and she has never heard the phrase before.

—It means, darling, that although the phantom pain is undoubtedly real to you, the causes are more psychogenic now than physiological, what we call a functional pain. Don't look so insulted, sweetie, I'm not saying you're deranged nor that you're malingering. Malingering is very rare in this field. But some patients, who are depressive or hysterical, unconsciously prolong their symptoms even for years and years, and suffer genuine agonies that in the end can only be dealt with by sympathectomy, which is not as you might think darling, don't look so frightened, the removal of sympathy but the removal of certain nerves or rather ganglia in the sympathetic autonomous nervous system, a small local operation. But you don't want more surgery do you, or, for that matter, a leucotomy, that's much more drastic.

—What! Never.

—Well, there you are. That's by way of a playful threat darling since you're not in fact either depressive or hysterical but a normal healthy girl who's had a nasty shock and a nasty operation. Would you like another course of electroencephalic treatment? That gave you some relief, didn't it?

—No.

—Well, there's a new thing called white sun, a nice poetic name for audio-analgesia, it's fed into the ear over such a range of auditory stimuli it swamps all the receptors in the brain—

—Shut up!

—I was hoping you'd say that. All right darling, calm down. You want to deal with this yourself. You're a good brave girl. doing very well with the new artificial limb, I hear from physiotherapy. That's quite comfortable, isn't it? Doesn't hurt? Good. And are you occupying your mind?

—Yes.

—Good. What with?

—Oh, thoughts. Ideas.

—Now that's not so good. You mustn't get ideas. What thoughts? You should do something. Prepare for ordinary life. We'll be discharging you soon and you must think of that.

—You just told me thoughts are not so good.

—Smart girl, you'll be all right. Do you have a job you can go back to?

—I was a model.

—Oh. I'm sorry sweetie, you did tell me and so did your mother. Yes. I forgot for a moment.

—You have so many patients.

—That's no excuse.

—As a matter of fact I thought, perhaps, I could write.

—To whom, darling?

—Just, write. You know, novels.

—Oh yes. Love stories you mean? Or spies? Why not, there's a lot of money in it. As long as you don't get too excited yourself, tension brings back the phantom you know.

—Well, I wasn't exactly thinking of love stories no she isn't exactly thinking of love stories or spies although I love her and I spy on her through the symptoms which she cherishes a little for the soft-voiced and sexy-eyed sympathy of the internuncial pool in the spinal cord or in other words my dear my little girl my love my good sweet little girl the higher sensory centres with resulting summation of abnormal stimuli and a persistence of the pain pattern she cherishes due to higher-level involvement fear of sympathectomy and white sun swamping all receptors in her brain. She is thinking of me to write about in order to get me out of her system as they call it not sympathetic or parasympathetic autonomous but cerebrospinal out of her midbrain on to paper instead of aching there fifty-three and a half centimetres away from her stump now circumscribed mature and non-proliferating with a phantom lower leg between though painless but undoubtedly projecting out the pain of sharp nails driven into the metatarsus and the ball of the foot that only exists in the higher sensory centres near the optic thalamus with which she sees me in her inner eye visio-erotically lateral to the aqueduct of Sylvius in the region of the pain pathways until I exist again so strong so hypertrophied and so sensuously detailed that I galvanise my impulses up the free nerve-terminations of her pain fibres afferent proprioceptive and she starts moaning like an animal or a woman in joy ineffable.

I shall not let her get rid of me with words that recreate my shape my galvanising atoms of agony on mere paper to be read by careless unsuffering millions vicariously and thus dispersed. I shall possess her and possess her again obsessing her absorbing her growing strong on her distress that excites me and recreates my shape as her sweet phantom foot with its associated pain intractable unendurable and cherished.

She writes however. She has a biro pen and a small exercise book Denis brought her. He got off with a broken arm worn in a sling for a while and looked like Napoleon short podgy oddly continental with a thin straight wisp from his receding hair down over his brow but constantly smoothed back and patted down as he says how are you dear and the brow contracts a little with guilt concern embarrassment fear removing the sympathy and any love that might have been with two legs. She uses him but not so much as well she might and he brings her fruit and flowers and books she wants about amputation syndromes not magazines full of models and the biro pen and the small exercise book that stays closed and empty for some time as I continue to possess her again and again growing huge on her distress that excites me in increasing rhythm and recreates my shape and my obsession with her aching my desire. Despite the increasing rhythm however or because of I need the rest-periods to withdraw my atoms after detumescence before gathering them up into the neuroblasts that will formulate me anew within her brain along the spinothalamic tract and the efferent fibres and she opens meanwhile the small exercise book and in thin impersonal strokes she writes the words she hears like white sun swamping all other receptors in the brain so that the white page slowly engraves itself with the victim to be haunted is female. And beautiful. This makes a difference. She has the habit of confidence, but also a greater adjustment to achieve while I slumber rest in my detumescence. She betrays me.

She isn't thinking of a love-story spy-thriller although she loves me spies on me through the symptoms cherished nor a novel no Proust she à la recherche du pied perdu I also like my little joke I can make cleverer ones than Mr. Poole but she starts humbly with a short story that says the victim is female and very beautiful as she knows very well with open eyes that can bring beauty alive with awareness of pain terror despair or anger, not to mention desire and liquid tenderness or even the alluring invitation down the pathways of pain swamped by the white sun of the words she hears, their nuclear cells radiating from the cochlear ganglion of the interior ear in the temporal lobe and round the cerebral cortex to the visual centre in the occipital lobe where the optic chiasm turns me and her whole body upside down until relayed into the parietal lobe and ending in the thalamus where contact pain heat cold localisation discrimination recognition of posture merge with the power of responding to different intensities of stimuli so that I drown in merely abstract existence feel knocked out in percussion and bombarded till my imitation unmyelated nerve-fibres degenerate curl up and die.

It is a proven scientific fact that women have a higher pain threshold than men. Which makes the task more difficult but interesting. All right, let her continue I can bide my time in detumescence until she exhausts herself and begs me to return or recreates me anew out of the tension from fatigue and emptiness. For even within that distinction the threshold varies from subject to subject and from time to time and there is rhythm in the haunting game as in any other according to stress drugs distraction violent activity including sex and literary creation as with a soldier in combat all senses occupied unaware of wound until his wild ferocity is abated. For there are ways to recreate distress. The electroencephalic treatment she has now prescribed herself may merely alter the nature of the pain and the position of the phantom limb. What fools they are. Variety of position is the spice of intimacy. I find it very exciting. Despite the annihilation through merely abstract existence on the rapidly neuroblasted paper there are still ways of lowering the threshold. Severe mental deprivation for example raises it and the highly intelligent undoubtedly suffer more than the plethoric unimaginative which she certainly is not being at the moment. She thinks about me, thus creating my shape her phantom foot, visually, aurally in words and sensuously in bones flesh skin and neuroblasts that dance along the axis cylinders within the myelin-sheathed fibres of the foot that isn't there except on paper to be read by careless unsuffering millions vicariously and thus dispersed.

I had existed so strong so hypertrophied and so cellularly detailed that her abstract creation will be the death of me unless the electroencephalic treatment she has prescribed herself merely alters my nature my position more or less distant from the stump as a projection of the central body-image in the higher sensory centres in excitatory state galvanising my impulses into the free nerve-terminations of her pain fibres that tingle afferent proprioceptive and the imitation neurones I am recomposed of agitate their dendrites like mad ganglia arborising the system as the cell-bodies dance along the fibres of the foot that isn't there, move backwards now, tugging away from the interlaced antennae as if trying to wrench themselves of some submicroscopic umbilical tie anchored into soft tissue, caught in bone, straining to freedom birth and terror of time and space as the neuroblasts race down the fibrils and create me, shape me and I ache strongly I swell to huge existence that possesses her wholly and loves her loves her loves and hurts her unendurably until she moans and pants like an animal or a woman in joy ineffable and the cortical areas respond by switching off the supply of blood along the nerves leaving the spinal cord and out she passes out.

She looks so beautiful, so white and ashen pale in all that ashen hair like dead nerve-fibres that conduct no pain but sheath the white face peaceful now with conjugate upward gaze vanished beyond the slit eyelids to face the darker phantoms of the womb the tomb the cavern the ebb and flow of internuncial pools linked to the chasm of death and timelessness that draws her like a magnet from the moment of the fall wrench of umbilical muscle rough manhandling tumbling lying in soft tissue sucking at heaven severed weight of body on crumbling legs and fall through days and minutes. Eyes open can bring archetypes alive and love that draws me like a magnet from the moment of my rebirth in desire to recreate my shape her phantom foot and devastate her beauty with my aching hugeness as an intractable phantom pain.

Yes, there are ways to recreate distress, less often perhaps, which is the way of intimacy and even haunting has its rhythm decreasing increasing according to stress fatigue drugs general constitution previous equilibrium distraction violent activity including sex and writing. I shall learn to be more discreet, play hard to get perhaps but only play. I cannot live without her and I know her weakness now, I know she needs my love my presence my shape her slim long phantom foot with its concomitant hugeness as a phantom pain.

She cries quietly now. I find this very exciting.

The Needle Man and the Scent Maker

The Scent Maker has a feeling that the Needle Man will be in an angry mood. Relatively angry, for a sage.

The waiting room is almost as smelly as it is dark, for there are human beings, and the waiting is long, and the day is hot, and the plane trees on that side of the house shut out the dazzling sun. The waiting room is chilly and dark, but the chill and the dark seem only to preserve, dankly, each individual hot smell which the human beings bring from outside, in hidden recesses. The Scent Maker closes his eyes.

'Dear God I thank you and the Needle Man that I can still smell the bad smells. But dear, dear God and please Needle Man let me not lose the good smells for ever. And ever Amen.'

The Needle Man isn't even there yet, '*Il accouche*,' his secretary has said as if he were Zeus, and the Scent Maker sees him in a mind's eye bubble, giving birth out of his head or thigh to a dreamy female in gauze and little else, other than the perfume she advertises. The mind's eye bubble bursts. The Needle Man is famous as the best midwife in the region. He does it with needles. He is much in demand therefore, and a difficult birth can scatter his schedule for days.

Tyres growl suddenly up the gravel of the drive and screech to a stop. In the dark room the round and the long, the bilious and the sanguine, the young and the old faces, placid from waiting, light up with varied hopes of loving attention. Doubt flickers also. Is it the doctor, or merely another patient?

He storms through to his consulting room with a wild *bonjour* thrown at the circle of reproachful or expectant eyes. A well-dressed woman is already on her feet and follows him in, clanking shut the big double doors, first one and then the other.

'Our appointment was for two-thirty,' says a thin girl to the closing door and then to the room in general. 'We've been here an hour and a half.'

'You are together?' The Scent Maker hopefully addresses a weedy youth next to the girl. The youth plunges a furiously blushing face into his comic strip and the thin girl gives a tinkling laugh.

'I'm with my mother. Our appointment was for two-thirty. We've been here since—'

'*Moi tre*,' says a large old lady in black. '*Solamente una puntura*.'

'My daughter's lost her whole afternoon at the lycée.' The mother of the thin girl opens wide her hairy nostrils.

'*Tre. Ma . . . solamente una puntura*.'

'But, Madame, we are all here for a *puntura*,' says the Scent Maker. 'It's a new vice. Like dope.' He gestures with an imaginary injection on his outstretched arm, mocking a desperate look. Then he laughs nervously.

'*Si, si. Tre. Sono le quattro*.'

'My other little boy's been first in arithmetic ever since the doctor started treating him.' A sallow woman in the corner holds a meagre child with an enormous head and vacant eyes. 'Now this one wants it too.' The head seems almost to topple over in anticipation.

'Let me see, then, if the lady who's just gone in was for two, then he's two hours late. My appointment was for three-thirty so I should get in at five-thirty.'

'Ours was for two-thirty,' says the thin girl. 'We've been here nearly two hours.'

But the doctor is cutting short the consultations. The well-dressed woman comes out and the thin girl goes in, followed by her mother's hairy nostrils.

The Scent Maker starts examining noses. He is very nose-conscious. The youth hidden in the comic strip clearly has adenoids. The pink nose of an elderly gentleman opposite twitches as if longing for a pinch of snuff. The child who wants to be first in arithmetic picks his and carefully examines its content before eating it. The Italian old lady sniffs deeply.

'Dear God and Needle Man save my sensitive nose.' The Scent Maker prays, and it passes the time, prayer being made elastic by obsessive visitations.

The overpowering scent of jasmine below his window, one night, ceases to overpower. More than that it is simply not there. In anguish he steps out into the moonlight which seems to have drunk up the scent of jasmine. He walks down to the field and bends over the plants. They are covered with small white flowers, but the flowers have no scent. He stares balefully at the moon.

He cannot sleep. At dawn he hears the voices of the jasmine pickers. Then silence as they scatter about the field. And the memory of Angèle.

'Angèle my love, when can we get married?'

'Well, first there is the rose, and then there is the jasmine.'

'And after that the orange flower. But Angèle, this'll go on for ever. Don't you understand you needn't go picking at all if you marry me? I'm a highly paid executive. I'm the Man-of-Ideas, you see.'

'And what about my television?'

'But Angèle, even the cinema hurts my eyes, then I can't smell.'

'Well but if you won't buy me a television then I must.'

'Angèle my love, of course I'll buy you a television.'

'You will? Ah then we can get married soon, between the rose and the jasmine.'

'But you won't be picking jasmine if we get married.'

Between the rose and the jasmine comes a great flower of blood on the road and Angèle never picks the jasmine again. Or the rose.

There are voices again in the field. A strident country voice and a male voice. It is Madame Guarini glad to straighten her back for a chat with the grocer on his early morning round. The conversation seems to go on for ever. He cannot hear the words, only the stridency and the male murmur. The distilled essence of Madame Guarini is stridency, just as the extracted absolute of jasmine is Angèle. The silence of Angèle for ever. '*Bon. Allez.*' Ah, this means goodbye. No. The conversation starts again. Perhaps they are saying that the jasmine smells good. Or strident as a factory siren. And how will he continue to bluff at the fact-ory? '*Bon Allez. Au revoir.*' But the conversation is renewed. The light is also strident, through the shutters. The sky must be as blue as every day. The Southern accents jerk up and down like whiffs from the fact-ory extractors. '*Bon Allez.*' This time it really is over.

He gets up and walks down to the field in his pyjamas. Colourful backs and straw hats interrupt the green, which is still much dotted with white.

'Good morning. Big harvest today?'

'Oh yes, the night's been busy. Hot already, isn't it?'

'Tell me, Madame Guarini, can you smell the scent as you pick?'

'Oh, you know, I'm so used to it, I wouldn't smell God Himself if He chose to hide in a jasmine flower.'

'Ah, yes, maybe that's what it is.'

'*Bon. Allez.*'

'*Allez.*'

At the factory the vans bring in the innumerable baskets of jasmine from all over the region. From the gallery he can see the baskets move along the conveyor belt like planets in their orbits. The sickly odour of mingled essences and aromatic chemicals permanently pervades the whole factory and the area half a mile around. He knows this. But he cannot smell it.

'That's what it is. After all I caught the dung driving past the Bartolo farm.'

He enters the laboratory, a very library of bottles. The white-over-alled men move here and there between the shelved stacks. His office and the Scent Maker's Organ Room are at the other end. He sits at the Scent Makers organ and stares at the horse-shoe of narrow shelves lined with vials. Beside the milligram scale in the centre of the horse-shoe, his assistant has already prepared the vial with the result of the scent created yesterday. A soupçon of new leather, a touch of burnt grass, a pinch of fennel. And the jasmine. His nostrils tremble on the brink. There is no smell.

'Oh, you know, I'm so used to it I wouldn't smell God Himself if He chose to hide in a vial.'

'A bit of a cold perhaps . . .'

' . . . So you see, doctor, it can't be just a cold.'

The consulting room is full of smoke and he waves a passage for his sensitive nose. Before sitting down he has sniffed at the large bouquet of red carnations that protects the Needle Man from the anxiety of his patients. He has smelt nothing.

'I've had six acupunctures on the nose and I'm no better.'

'Six. I've done six already? So I have.'

The Needle Man stares at a file as if it were a very abstruse poem.

'Yes. Two at the top and four here on the left nostril. And doctor, only the smells I don't want to smell remain. Why?'

The Scent Maker leans forward, hitting the desk so that the carnations shudder, then back swiftly as if the desk had itself emitted one of those unwanted smells, which the Needle Man promptly makes visible with a ring of smoke. But the Needle Man is still lost in the file. The Scent Maker suddenly notices that he looks grey with fatigue.

'Doctor, have you eaten any lunch?'

Surprised gratitude gleams for a moment in the doctor's eyes. But his harsh tone quenches it.

'No.'

The Scent Maker is silent. He wants to tell the Needle Man to go and eat. I can wait, he wants to say. But the reversal of solicitude embarrasses him. He doesn't really wish to break the comfortable rigidity of the professional relationship, which at once reimposes itself, for the Needle Man is already in the examination room.

'Come this way.'

The Scent Maker is again the patient. After all he has waited two hours.

'You see, doctor, I am the Man-of-Ideas. What would I do—'

'Sit down. No. Here.'

'I don't think it's just a cold because—'

'Take off your trousers.'

'My trousers?'

But the Needle Man merely looks agonised, with head thrown back and eyes closed to the removal of the trousers, as if seeking a diagnosis far back in his memory. And the Scent Maker is lost in admiration for the Needle Man, who reputedly always finds an ultimate cause in a completely different part of the body.

'It makes illness exciting and mysterious,' he tells him. 'Most doctors won't see beyond the organ of their speciality. Ouch.'

'It's tender there, is it? And here?'

'No.'

'Here?'

'No.'

'Hmmm. Pull up your trousers.'

The Needle Man says this in a disgusted tone, and the Scent Maker feels hurt.

'That woman!' says the Needle Man looking down the Scent Maker's throat.

'What woman?'

'Don't talk. Say "Ah".'

'Ah . . . What woman?'

'Take off your tie . . . That first woman. I lashed out at her.'

'The one in childbirth?'

'No, of course not. Can you hear when I do this?

'Hear what?'

'Hmmm. Six o'clock. I'll have to tonify the opposite.'

'You said: Six o'clock I'll have to tonify the opposite.'

'Good. Your right foot, please.'

The Scent Maker silently thanks God and the Needle Man that he is not going deaf as well. To make sure he asks politely:

'Do you mean the Italian?'

'No. That first one who rushed in after me.'

The Scent Maker jumps as the needle jabs, it seems, into the bone itself just below the inside ankle.

'What's the matter?'

'It hurts.'

'Good. I like it when it hurts. No, but can you imagine, she rushes in and pours out her pains and woes before I have time to sit down.' For once it is the Needle Man who searches the eyes of his patient for a reaction. 'So I said not a word. I went to my cupboard, helped myself to a glass of port, brought it to the desk, lit a cigarette, and drank. Then I said, "Right, now you may begin." Really, the selfishness of some people, it's unbelievable.'

The Scent Maker is silent again. He has never seen the Needle Man so animated. He wants to say, 'Doctor, why don't you go and eat something? I can wait.' But it is pointless now. The Needle Man seems to sense the question and looks hard at the sand falling through the small glass-timer.

'What organ are you reaching now?' the Scent Maker asks instead, staring at the gold needle which the Needle Man is slowly rotating on his inner ankle. 'Is it for the sense of smell?'

'For the moment no.'

'For the what?'

'Hmmm?'

'I thought you mentioned an organ. I asked you—'

'No.' The last grain of sand has fallen through the timer and the Needle Man removes the gold needle. Eyes closed, he seeks a diagnosis far back in his memory. 'Pull down your trousers please.'

'Again? I mean—'

'I want your stomach.'

'Doctor, shall I recover my sense of smell? You see, I'm the Man-of-Ideas and—'

'Lie there.' The Needle Man unrolls a tape-measure and carefully marks a distance from the thorax with his finger. 'How's your little boy?'

'Glued to the television. Are you going to make me a new suit?'

'A new person, probably. Madame your wife is responding nicely, isn't she?'

'Oh, she's become a real needle-addict. Ouch! Must have her regular punctures. You're a monkey on her back I tell her. What's this one for?'

He adds shyly.

'General relaxation. It's a beauty, this one, I'm very fond of it.'

'Aren't you going to do one for the sense of smell?

'For the moment no.'

'Oh, I see. For the moment, no. I thought—'

He tails off as the doctor's eyelids close then get hidden behind his open hand. The Scent Maker feels sleepy. The silence is full of imagined odours, but he can see only their symptoms. A jar of ambergris. A vial. The fennel, the fresh leather, the field of white flowers. He couldn't smell God Himself hidden in a flower, between the jasmine and the rose. *Allez. Nous plus au bois, les lauriers sont coupés.* But the planets revolve. The Scent Maker asks, quietly:

'Why was it such a difficult birth?'

'An exhausted woman,' says the Needle Man without moving his eyes from his hand, or his other hand from the needle that is activating a mysterious meridian.

'Too many children?'

The Needle Man lifts his head and shrugs.

'That's life.'

Then he adds dreamily:

'Life is worth everything.'

'What did you do?'

'I gave her strength.'

'Like this?'

'And otherwise.'

There is tobacco on the Needle Man's breath, which travels on a faint aroma of port surrounded with ether. Add cinnamon, styrax, bergamot oil, extracted absolute of carnation. The Scent Maker's nostrils quiver.

'*Bon*,' says the Needle Man.

'*Allez.*'

'I beg your pardon?'

'Nothing.'

'Well, pull up your trousers.'

He uses the same tone of disgust but the Scent Maker is not hurt.

'Doctor,' he says when they are back in the consulting room, 'I think I can smell your carnations.'

'Not yet. At least, it won't last. You'll feel exalted for an hour. But make another appointment.'

'Well, anyway, I've invented a new scent.'

'*Sans blague.*'

The Needle Man is filling in an index card and doesn't seem in the least interested. The consultation is over. Probably the boy with adenoids is next. Or the child who wants to be first in arithmetic too.

'Doctor.' The Scent Maker would like to prolong the interview, to show his gratitude, to make a friend of the Needle Man. 'I will call it after you.'

'They all say that.'

'Oh.' The Scent Maker is embarrassed again by this reminder of the Needle Man's busy life. He asks nervously: 'Are you going to eat now?'

'Not yet.'

The Needle Man stretches out his hand. The Scent Maker takes it with a deep breath as if testing a perfume, which he exhales slowly.

'Perhaps I'll call it Angélique,' he whispers.

'*Bon. Alors—*'

'No,' says the Scent Maker on his way out, 'Angélique is precisely what I won't call it.'

'Next please,' says the Needle Man's voice behind him and the old gentleman with the twitchy nose rises painfully on arthritic limbs. Clearly it is not his nose he is consulting the doctor about.

The waiting room is darker than ever. And chillier. Several new patients have arrived, bringing in cooler smells as the heat outside has lightened. The secretary bends her head over the appointments book and he catches the banality of Chanel No. 5.

'Yes,' says the Scent Maker as he steps out into the fragrant summer evening, 'I shall call it "Needling No. 7".'

Red Rubber Gloves

From this position on my high balcony, the semi-detached beyond the garden looks more squat than it ought to in such a prosperous suburb, forming with its Siamese twin a square inverted U that faces me and boxes a wide inverted T of a backyard, neatly divided by a hedge of roses and hydrangeas. On the left of the hedge there is a bit of lawn. On the right, only a small paved yard. The house on the left seems devoid of life, devoid, that is, of the kind of life liable to catch the eye and stop it in its casual round, mutating its idle curiosity through momentary fascination and hence, inexorably, by the mere process of reiteration, to a mild but fixed obsessiveness. As does the right-hand house.

In the angle of the square U, outside the french windows of the right-hand house, the girl sits on the edge of the red canvas bed in a pale pink bikini, carefully oiling inch after inch of her thin white body. She looks, from up here, totally naked, the pink bikini being so pale, and she sits on the edge of the red canvas bed which is set obliquely in the paved yard to face the morning sun. She has oiled the arms, the shoulders, the chest and the long midriff. Now she is doing the right leg, starting with the foot, the ankle, then the shin, as if to meet her upper oily self halfway. She is oiling the right thigh. Inside the thigh. The left foot. If the heat wave holds out she will perhaps become brown enough to con-trast with the pink and so look less totally naked on the red canvas bed. The inside of the left thigh. She lies now framed in the red canvas bed, chin up eyes closed to face the hot June sun. Round the corner from her naked body, at the square end of the inverted U, the red rubber gloves lie quiet on the kitchen windowsill.

In the morning the large rectangular windows of the house tend to reflect the sun in some at least of their thirty-two small black squares framed in cream-painted wood. And in the afternoon they are quite cast into the shade as the sun moves round to face me on my high balcony, immobilised in convalescence. I cannot therefore see much further than the beginning of the pink washbasin in the bathroom or, in the kitchen below it, the long and gleaming double-sink unit. And the red rubber gloves, moving swiftly apart and together, vanishing and reappearing, moving apart and down. All the windows of both houses, those of the kitchen and of the bathroom above it, at each end of the square inverted U, and those of each bedroom inside the U above the french windows, are rectangular and divided into four panels, each of eight black squares, two over two over two over two, all in cream-painted frames.

The thin girl has melted away into the sun, the red canvas bed is empty.

At least, that is presumably also the layout of the bathroom and kitchen in the left-hand house, for the windows are mostly hidden by the apple-tree. The houses are almost identical, except for the lawn on the left of the hedge. In the backyard of the right-hand house, a clothes-line stretches from the high wooden fence to one end of the kitchen window, and another from the same spot in the high wooden fence to the other end, forming a V with the first clothes line.

The girl, the daughter of the house, is perhaps aware that I am watching it, for the bathroom curtains have been hastily drawn. On closer scrutiny I can see that the bathroom in fact occupies only two of the framed panels in the upper window, the right-hand two, the curtains of which have been hastily drawn and are lined in white. The other two must belong to a small bedroom, the girl's bedroom perhaps. Its curtains, pulled back on either side, have a buff lining. It is midday and the cool sun of a cold July tries to pierce through the greyness to warm me in my convalescence. I call it convalescence because the doctor does and the sun is trying to shine, but I know that the paralysis will not retreat, rather will it creep up, slowly perhaps but inexorably over the years, decades even, until it reaches the vital organs.

In the kitchen window of the right-hand house, one of the panels of two squares over two over two is open to reveal a black rectangle and the beginning of the gleaming sink. Inside the sink is a red plastic bowl and on the windowsill are the red rubber gloves, now at rest.

The morning sunlight slants on all the windows, reflecting gold in some of the black squares but not in others, making each rectangular window, with its eight squares across and four squares down, look like half a chessboard gone berserk to confuse the queen and all her knights. The bathroom window and the kitchen window below it form two halves of a chessboard, more or less.

In the black rectangle of the open kitchen window the sunlight gleams on the stainless steel double-sink unit, just beyond the cream-painted frame. Above the gleaming sink the red rubber gloves move swiftly, rise from the silver greyness lifting a yellow mass, plunging it into greyness, lifting it again, twisting its tail, shifting it to the right-hand sink, moving back left, vanishing into greyness, rising and moving swiftly, in and out, together and apart.

On closer scrutiny I can see that in the left-hand house the wooden frames of the thirty-two black squares, eight by four in each of the rect-angular windows, are painted white. It is only the right-hand house which has cream-painted windows. They all looked the same behind the trees against the strong August sun that faces me on my high balcony. The left-hand house seems quite devoid of life. Possibly the two rectan-gular windows one above the other in the left-hand house, are not the windows of the bathroom and kitchen at all. It is difficult to see them through the apple-tree, and of course the goldening elm in the garden at the back of my block of flats. In the right-hand house, however, the lower room is definitely the kitchen, in the black rectangle of which the red rubber gloves move swiftly apart, shake hands, vanish into grey-ness, lift up a foam-white mass, vanish and reappear, move to the right, move back, plunge into greyness, rise and move swiftly right. Beyond the red rubber gloves is a pale grey shape, then blackness.

Despite so much washing activity and two clotheslines in the back-yard I have not seen the woman yet, the mother of the girl. Surely, she must come out one day to hang out the washing on the line. I have not seen the woman yet, or the girl again, only the red rubber gloves, although the woman has been washing ceaselessly day after day since I first began to watch the house. She must have a large family, which likewise I have not seen, except for the girl sunbathing in that June heatwave, oiling her body inch by inch, lying it seemed quite naked on the red canvas bed. But as I stare at the empty clothesline, I know with a mild pang that I have seen shirts hanging from it, and slips, and night-dresses, many a time, without then registering the image, which only now recurs very precisely in the back of my memory. Yet I have never seen the woman herself come out to hang the washing. She must do it while I am having physiotherapy, or seeing the doctor, or eating a meal. Perhaps she waits for a moment when I am not on the balcony, to come out and hang her washing.

On the stainless steel draining board just inside the black rectangle of the open kitchen window is a red mass on a white plate. One of the red rubber gloves unfolds the mass, the other holds a carving knife, almost invisible in the redness of the glove, and cuts the meat into small square pieces on a pale blue chopping board, carefully removing the gristle. In red rubber gloves. A bit much, really. The left red rubber glove sweeps the gristle into the gleaming sink, and then moves up and down, quickly pushing, presumably, the gristle down the unit. One of the red rubber gloves holds the edge of the stainless steel sink, the other moves quickly all around it.

There is no doubt about it, now that the strong September sun has dimmed and gone behind a cloud, the window frames and the frames of all the small black squares inside the windows of the left-hand house are painted white. And the window frames and the frames of the small black squares in the windows of the right-hand house are painted cream.

The red rubber gloves are upstairs now, in the white washstand just beyond the cream-painted squares of the right-hand house. It is very exciting when they are upstairs. They move apart and vanish, rise and come together, shake hands, vanish and reappear. They look larger in the small washbasin. The shape behind is white in the rosy darkness and the arms above the gloves are clearly visible. It is a rosy darkness due to the walls being probably painted pink. Inside it must be quite light. The arms are thin and white. The red rubber gloves have been removed, the wrists dip naked into the pink washbasin, one hand soaps the other arm, under the arm, the neck, the other hand soaps the first arm, under the arm, the neck.

The stainless steel is dull today, the bright reflecting squares have become black squares, removing the uneven permutations of sunlight on the two halves of the chessboard. The red rubber gloves move swiftly apart, rise from the greyness lifting a red mass, vanish and reappear. The arms above the gloves are thin and white. Despite so much washing activity I have not seen the woman yet. But then I have not been out on the balcony for quite some time, it is too cold, even with rugs. So I wheel my chair by the dining room window and watch. Surely the woman must one day emerge to hang out all that tremendous wash. But no, the cold November drizzle is too cold and drizzly. Unless perhaps she has a spin dryer.

The woman steps out into the paved backyard holding in her thin white embrace the red plastic bowl full of wet clothes. She wears a black jumper and a short grey skirt, and the red rubber gloves. She is thin and has short hair. She puts down the basin and picks from it a shirt which she smooths out and hangs upon the line, upside down by the tails. And then another shirt. Then a pyjama top, with stripes. She and the girl who seemed totally naked on the red canvas bed are one and the same person.

Nobody moves at all in the house on the left. And yet the window corresponding to the bathroom and small bedroom window has one of its panels open. Through the denuded elm, books are visible on the extreme left wall.

The red rubber gloves move swiftly apart behind the cream-painted frames of the kitchen in the right-hand house. One of the squares reflects a pale December sun but otherwise all the squares are dark on the lower half of the chessboard. The red rubber gloves move swiftly apart, shake hands, vanish into a foam-grey mass, rise, vanish and reappear, move swiftly apart, vanish, rise, move apart, vanish, rise, move swiftly.

In the blackness beyond the gloves the shape is emerald green.

The woman has no daughter, and no washing machine. She is the daughter, she is the washing machine. She is probably the spin dryer too. Whoever she washes for so continually is never to be seen, from this position at my high dining room window in the immobility of my convalescence. The two houses have separate roofs, high and deeply sloping in a late Edwardian style with neat little, tight little tiles of darkened red.

The red rubber gloves are also worn to chop up meat on the pale blue chopping board. A bit much, really. The meat must taste of stale detergent. The left red rubber glove sweeps the gristle into the gleaming sink, and then moves up and down pushing the gristle down the presumably waste disposal unit. One of the red rubber gloves holds the edge of the stainless steel sink, the other moves swiftly around it.

It is three o'clock in the afternoon and the wintry sun accuses my impotence with blank undazzling orange in a dull white sky. The thin white shape appears at the bedroom window, draws the buff-lined curtains with swift brusquery. This is the first time I have seen the woman relaxing. At least, I assume she is relaxing since she has drawn the curtains. It was so jerkily done. Staring at the drawn buff curtains I know that I have seen them drawn before, without registering the image. No doubt in June already, during the heatwave, she went up to the bedroom at three o'clock in the afternoon and drew the curtains swiftly, jerkily, in a great hurry to relax while I was dozing off. Perhaps she is not relaxing. All I saw was a quick white shape, a slip maybe, unless it was an overall, although her arms were bare. In the kitchen she sometimes wears a white overall, which makes her stand out better against the darkness of the rectangle. And of course the red rubber gloves. They lie at rest now on the kitchen windowsill just inside the small black squares, while she relaxes, thinking of black velvet or of restful landscapes as she isolates her head, and then dismisses it as she isolates her neck, and then dismisses it as she isolates her left shoulder, her left arm, flowing, flowing, out, her right arm, and then dismisses it as she isolates her left leg, and her left foot, and then dismisses it as she isolates her right leg, her right foot. That is what the physiotherapist tells me to do when I am in pain. Normal people have to do it all the way down, isolating the left leg, then the right, but I feel no pain down there at all, my legs have isolated themselves, so there's no point. It is the neck and shoulders, and the back especially, that ache. Perhaps she isolates the inside of her thigh.

The curtains are drawn open swiftly and a white shape moves away. A quick relaxation, that, merely counting to a hundred maybe, with a hundred deep breaths.

The thin white shape appears behind the cream-framed squares of the bathroom window. Briefly, for the white lined curtains are drawn with a brusque movement.

On closer scrutiny the bathroom curtains are not lined in white, but are made of plastic, the reverse side of which is white. Unless perhaps they have replaced, quite recently, the earlier bathroom curtains with the white cotton lining. It is now impossible to tell. There is a faint pink and blue pattern, ducks, possibly, or boats, brighter no doubt on the inside. Six out of thirty-two black squares reflect the pale December morning sun, Castle top left, Bishop left, White Queen on her colour, pawn one advanced two paces, pawn two advanced one pace, pawn four immobilised in dire paralysis.

The lower half of the chessboard reflects no sun. In the black rectangle of the kitchen window the red rubber gloves move swiftly apart. One of the gloves holds the edge of the stainless steel sink, the other moves swiftly around it. Three shirts are hanging on the line, upside down, and a pyjama top, male underpants, one nightie, two slips, three panties and a pale green blouse. There are no pyjama trousers.

Snow covers the two steep roofs, and all the trees and gardens. The narrow bricks of the Siamese twin houses seem unnaturally dark. The backyards look alike, no lawn now on the left, only the apple tree, bare branched in black and white. The snow piles high on the windowsills of the left-hand house. But on the right-hand house the windowsills have been swept clean and stand out dark and grey. The light is on in the kitchen, the woman clearly visible, in a blue smock over a red polo neck.

The red rubber gloves move swiftly apart, plunge into greyness and bring out a plate, a cup, another plate, another, and a saucepan, after scouring.

The snow makes map-like patterns on the dark red and steeply sloping roofs.

The red rubber gloves move swiftly apart above the gleaming sink in the dark rectangle of the open kitchen window. The April sun slants on the small black squares, whitening a few and leaving others blank, like half a chessboard gone berserk in order to confuse the queen and all her knights.

During my relapse I have thought a lot about the woman. I was unable to sit by the window but I saw her clearly in my mind's eye. Busy, always busy in her red rubber gloves. But I know. Clearly she has a lover. She receives him at three o'clock in the afternoon and swiftly draws the curtains. There is so little time.

At three o'clock in the afternoon I sit by the dining room window now and watch the house. The lover is there, behind the curtains, caressing her face, and then her neck, her breasts, her belly and the inside of her thigh as she lies totally naked on the red counterpane. Her belly is enormous for she is eight and a half months pregnant by him. She must have been getting bigger and bigger during my relapse, and of course before, although at that time it wouldn't have been so noticeable from this position at my dining room window. Therefore he cannot make love to her but he caresses her. She loves me manually and I am content.

The tiny baby lies dead on the pale blue chopping board by the stainless steel sink. She cuts him up with the big carving knife and drops the small bits one by one into the waste disposal unit which growls and grinds them into white liquid pulp.

The red rubber gloves move swiftly apart, half lost in all the blood. One hand holds the edge of the stainless steel sink, the other moves quickly around it.

The heatwave is tremendous for late May. The woman sits on the edge of the red canvas bed in her pale pink bikini, carefully oiling her body inch by inch, the arms, the shoulders, the chest and the long midriff. Now she is doing the right leg, the shin, the thigh, the inside of the thigh. She lies on the red canvas bed, thin, white and totally naked in her invisible bikini, chin up, eyes closed to face the morning sun that pours down melting her and my left side on my high balcony. In the black rectangle of the open kitchen window the yellow rubber gloves lie on the sill, at rest.

The Chinese Bedspread

The Chinese Bedspread

Not for three days after James—whom I never call Jim, even in bed—had spilt the Indian ink on the drab old tapestry bedspread did I say to him, unreproachfully:

'We shall have to get a new one.'

For it was I who had bumped into him as I turned brusquely from the chest of drawers with three of his shirts on my arm. My movements tend to be brusque, whereas he moves quietly as a cat. So how could I reproach him?

But a space of three days, which can remove all reproach from the mind and thereby from the voice, may also appear as a grudge-harbouring time to one who rarely listens to the mind behind the voice.

So that when I said,

'We shall have to get a new bedspread,' he looked startled, rather as if I had said, 'a new marriage bed', which was indeed possibly what I meant, but James is a clergyman and puts away such thoughts, if he has them.

Not that he is narrow-minded. Women taken in adultery he is quite Christ-like about, providing, I suppose, they do not include me. But he likes to cleanse temples, and has a thing about acquisitiveness, and affluence, and needles' eyes.

He does not like me to dream over advertisements in the glossies, which indeed do inevitably lead me into day-drifts about rich men's wives. His own spiritual journeys are infinitely more mysterious. He sets out on them at night, at least, late in the evening, round about my bedtime.

He said, 'But Penelope.' He never calls me Penny. At school I was always Plopsy, on account of my awkwardness. 'But Penelope, nobody comes in here, except us. And the room is so dark, the ink-stain could be a shadow. Or even part of the pattern.'

'It is true you don't see this room a great deal.' But there was no edge in my voice, for I was merely curious. 'What do you do downstairs, after I've gone to bed?'

Embarrassment flitted through his eyes and away, as if I had asked, do you practise levitation, and then it was immediately replaced by a look of thoughtfulness. But he didn't say I pray, or anything like that.

'Well, maybe you're right, but we can't just get rid of that bedspread. My mother gave it to us.'

'A dragon,' I said, 'I want something with a dragon. A scaly dragon breathing out flames and smoke, scarlet and gold and silvery grey. Chinese.' I breathed out the words like flames and smoke.

'You'll have to go to a very fancy shop for anything like that, Penelope.'

'But James, dear—'

'It is more for a Camel—'

'Perhaps a dragon is a bit much,' I conceded. 'But I would like something gorgeous, and shimmering. Orange or crimson, with golden branches twisting all over it like a dragon, the golden branches of a dragon tree. Or no, perhaps a magnolia tree in full bloom, on a background of pale eau-de-nil, yes, a magnolia tree, and birds of paradise perched on its outer branches, and a kingfisher below, where the rushes would grow in the silver ripples of water, and above, at the pillow end, all the pink and white magnolia flowers opening out into a flight of black and white swallows . . .'

I was admiring it in my mind's eye, which is prone to behold unattainable beauty. But the very detail made James decide that I was teasing him.

'You'll never find anything like that, Penelope.'

The salesmen raved monotonously about candlewick. All the bedspreads in the world seemed to be made of candlewick, lemon-yellow candlewick, lime-green candlewick, strawberry candlewick, sky-blue candlewick, white candlewick. We sell a lot of these, the salesmen said.

One day, James came home earlier than usual from the Calypso Youth Club, which is the love of his life apart from God and me, so that I was surprised. He looked both shaken and mysterious, acting as if he had seen, like Zacharias, a vision which conceivably concerned my future happiness. I felt a bit let down when he said, with muffled excitement,

'Penelope dear. I have brought you a bedspread.'

I tried quickly to put a wedge into my sinking feelings so that they might become rising ones, full of childlike surprise and joy.

'Oh, James! A bedspread?'

'Yes. You see, young Les Carter broke his guitar—someone fell on it during a fight the other day and bashed it in. Well, the club collected £2.17.9 and Les said he knew a place where he might pick up a guitar for about three pounds, in Willoughby Road, you know, where all those condemned houses are. There's a funny little junk shop on the corner there, do you know it, Penelope, it sells secondhand clothes as well, and it's called Mrs. Tibbs, Everything Bought and Sold. Well there it was in the window, the bedspread I mean, not the guitar—alas, there wasn't a guitar. It was hanging at the back, squashed out of sight by a large Victorian patchwork quilt. I saw it, you see—'

'James,' I said, turning alarm as best I could into breathless anticipation, 'Where is the bedspread?'

'Let me finish, dear. Well, she had no guitar, as I say, Mrs. Tibbs, a very pleasant woman indeed. She took it down, and with a—'

'James please. Where is it?'

'In the hall. In a brown . . . paper parcel.

'It's very dirty,' he called out in warning.

'But it only cost two pounds,' he went on as I brought it in and impatiently tugged the string over the corners of the parcel, then put them back with a sigh as I saw his frown and started working on the knots.

'She said she could have charged eight pounds if she had risked it with the cleaners. But she was sure it would clean all right.

'She said it needs mending a little, she put her heel through the side of it in the taxi. She said she could have charged twenty pounds if she hadn't done that.

'And of course, it needs, generally, seeing to . . .'

His voice tailed off as I at last unfolded the bedspread with a silken rustle and flung it open at his feet, like a Raleigh before the Queen.

'It's Chinese,' he murmured.

It was torn and grubby, and a riot of thick gold threads grew out of it like weeds, all over the place. But as I looked and looked, my mind's eye merged into my seeing eye and I recognised the bedspread I had described to James in that fit of unreproachful defiance. There was no dragon. The defiance had been too meek to get a dragon on a scarlet sheen. Nor were there birds of paradise, not even ruined ones. But it was made of shimmering pure silk in palest eau-de-nil, now blotched and patchy with dirt and mildew. And where the golden thread was still stitched down in close embroidery they made up twisted branches, bearing a kingfisher, quite unspoilt, in blues and cyclamen, that fluttered down after its mate, less bright in greens and browns. And higher up, the branches spread into great magnolia flowers, blossoming out of purple calyces, and higher still flew asymmetrically several swallows done in black and white long cross-threading, now loose like moulting feathers. The ripples below were also loose and broken up, and even the leaves and flowers and the legs of the kingfisher's mate needed stitching down, patiently, delicately, impossibly. But it was the golden dragonesque branches which were in the worst state. The whole design in fact was hardly clear, except to my mind's eye, which is prone to behold unattainable beauty.

But James had recognised it also. The beauty must therefore have existed.

'Tell me, Penelope, had you seen it? Did you ever pass that shop in Willoughby Road?'

'No, I've never been there.'

I examined the tear down the side.

'I'm afraid I can't mend it, you know. This tear alone would take me two days to darn, even if I could get enough silk and in that colour. And even so it ought to be done by invisible menders, who would charge the earth, and by the time we'd paid special prices to have it cleaned, it would hardly be a cheap bedspread. As to all this mass of loose gold thread—'

'Well, naturally,' he said, 'I wouldn't dream of going—'

'Stitching down all this loose embroidery, on this delicate Chinese silk, why it's impossible. I haven't the skill or the patience, or the time.'

'But it was so strange, Penelope, so very strange, seeing it there. Not quite seeing it, I mean, on account of the quilt, but guessing at it, then going in and the woman opening it out for me, just as you did now, with the same shuddering silk sound.'

I folded it up carefully.

'I don't find it so strange,' I said with some archness. 'You of all people should take the supernatural in your stride.'

He looked shocked.

'It's too trivial. Too pointless. What would it mean?'

'I don't know.'

But of course I did.

And so I sat, evening after evening, crinolined in the Chinese bedspread, bent over it in the lamplight as I patiently darned the tear with the finest silk I could find. Then I began stitching down the golden threads of a slim branch that fortunately twisted over the darn, making a good camouflage. The mended silk could hardly bear the weight of my stitches, despite my fine needle, but I strengthened it again from underneath as I sewed. There was a heavy hypnotism to the eye hidden in the delicate patterns, and soon I was following the gold threads one by one along the pencilled line still visible where the embroidery had got loose. Each gold thread was made of rice paper wrapped round with tinsel, and had to be stitched down with golden silk every two or three millimetres. My eyes ached and my back seemed to break. I went to bed each night feeling like an invalid, and only a small bit of branch or patch of silver water would begin to make sense each day.

And as I worked, the suitors dwelt in my mind, soldier, sailor, rich man, business executive, with their blandishments of silk, satin, muslin, terylene, courtelle, and smooth streamlined machines that surrounded me and were my servants, so that I could float in gauze and spend all my leisure making myself perfectly desirable and perfectly accomplished, for all these innumerable suitors. Or for James. Because that is what James says the advertisements in the glossies do. They arouse a woman's hidden desire to be the perfect mistress, he says, rather than the perfect wife.

I do not know whether James wants a perfect mistress. He never takes me with him on his own spiritual journeys.

At first he sat at his desk, and worked in silence, preparing his sermon, or writing letters to raise money for the Calypso Youth Club, or answering letters from the Probation Officer, or the Women's Guild, or parishioners, or revising his article on the *filioque* clause in the Creed. After a week he sat in his basket chair, reading, but watching me now and again between footnotes. The basket chair might well have creaked each time he lifted his eyes, I was so conscious of them.

'Penelope, how many suitors are inhabiting your mind as you stitch away?'

'Many,' I said, without looking up. 'Very many.'

Later he murmured again about the kingdom of heaven and the rich man and the eye of a needle, but I couldn't quite hear or for that matter grasp the exact analogy. I was not, after all, a camel.

But then he added, more audibly: 'The design is emerging quite clearly.

'It's very beautiful,' he said.

'Yes.' I had a little sob in my voice and could not elaborate the glories of the bedspread without perhaps crying. Instead, I muttered ungraciously, as if demanding praise, which I certainly needed: 'It's very difficult to stitch down without catching the lining.'

'It's astonishing' he said, 'it looks much cleaner already, now that the gold threads glitter close together as definite branches. It must be that the visibility of the design focuses the eye away from the dirt and the patchiness.'

Three weeks later I was working on the swallows. Our conversation, too, had taken wing, the air with pattern as the design became complete.

'I felt,' I said to James, 'as if you had been privately offered immortality by a beautiful nymph, in exchange for . . . well . . .'

'Conjugal distance?'

'That's not really what I meant. In exchange for destitution, rather, or—'

'Or poverty of spirit. Which is distance.'

'And then I felt as if the agreement had been quietly altered in some way so as to include my mind's eye, on certain conditions.'

'On condition that you accomplished some impossible task?'

Soon there only remained to be stitched down the silvery-grey feet of the kingfisher's less colourful mate. They looked more like wisps of smoke than bird's feet. The kingfisher himself, however, was flawless from foot to feathered crest.

'It's the most beautiful thing I've ever seen,' James said when the bedspread was laid out over the sitting room floor. My eyes ached and my back felt broken. The suitors had been chased out, the nymph's promise forgotten.

So I took the bedspread to the Textiles Museum, where a handsome young man examined it and told me it was a hundred years old, and advised me to take it to the Queen's cleaners. He too expressed the view that it was very beautiful, looking straight into my eyes.

'I'm glad it's old,' I said, 'I like old things.'

It looked exactly as I had first imagined it when it came back from the Queen's cleaners, shimmering and pale and subtly rich in tone. I spread it over the bed.

'Isn't it a bit too gorgeous, for us, I mean?'

'No, Penelope, it isn't. Not now.'

The next day I went along to Willoughby Road to tell Mrs. Tibbs how successful I had been with the Chinese bedspread she had sold to the vicar. I came upon the shop suddenly from round the corner. But the windows were empty of all patchwork quilts or old tweed suits or sequinned dresses, empty of saucepans, guitars and Coronation mugs. Above, the faded white letters still read 'Mrs. Tibbs, Everything Bought and Sold'. A Close-Down notice filled the door, giving no new address.

Dust filled the air as a solitary demolition worker hit the wall he was standing on, over the shop, against a roofless sky.

The Religious Button

The old woman stands on the threshold, so short that half the door-frame above her head is filled with the long cracked ceiling of the corridor in vanishing perspective beyond the bare grey bulb which hangs apparently over her like an amorphous dead small animal in fact outside room 32 as it swings slightly in the draught between the vanishing perspectives of the ceiling edges. Her wispy hair sticks out of a grey woolly cap. She looks blown out, fat and yet so pale she gives an impression of frailty. Perhaps she is about to have the breath of life slowly let out of her so that she will collapse to shrivelled rubber or maybe take off, like a tiered balloon, flying along the corridor a foot or so above the mottled lino and then higher as she passes by room 32, just missing the amorphous dead small animal, room 33 and up to the vanishing perspectives of the ceiling edges on and out of the broken window at the other end if she is rash enough to jettison the two battered suitcases that seem attached to her like weights on either side.

—No, I'm sorry, I don't want anything.

—Eh? You weren't listening, were you luv? I said I'm sorry to trouble you but would you be a dear and see if you've any old clothes you don't want. You dress ever so nice if I may say so though my eyes ain't as good as they used to be and I collect 'em you see.

—Oh. What is it for, UNICEF?

—What was that dear? You must forgive me, I'm a bit 'ard of 'earing.

—Just a minute. I'll go and see.

There is nowhere much to go however and little enough to see in the way of old clothes unwanted unless of course but no. Or yes not since charity begins at home the Lord will understand and if He changes His Mind again He will provide He did before.

The whitewood painted pink for a girl is full of small dresses, the summer cotton to the right the little red wool suit the blue velvet the pinafores the crisp white frock with roses round the rim. No. It's not possible. But what else is there? All other things are needed by the handmaid of the Lord the brown winter coat the black wool dress for mourning all that came and went the grey tweed skirt the blue maternity the pale blue cotton one for summer. All guarded at the back by the grey flannel trousers and the mould-coloured jacket of the man who came and went.

The second drawer contains underwear old but white and neat the blue jumper the grey cardigan the old orange sweater that would do it's out of tone for the waiting circumstance and in the third by itself the Nightdress of the Night. The fourth is full of baby clothes pink and white for a girl knitted socks thumb-to-fist-size clothes for two months and six, for one-year-old two and three, pants playsuits sleeping clothes eating clothes crying and laughing clothes but no, the gesture cannot be required. Or yes why not the Lord will understand that charity begins at home and if He changes His Mind again He will provide.

The bedclothes in the cot however will remain.

The old woman is still as short, the doorfrarne above her head still filled with the cracked ceiling in vanishing perspectives beyond the bare grey bulb that hangs like an amorphous dead small animal moving a little in the draught outside room 32. Her pale grey eyes light up at the surprising pile, the glazed look brightening momentarily.

—Oh you are good to me luv, God bless you dear, He-will-reward-you-never-fear.

—Not at all.

—What was that?

—I said, not at all.

—Oh but He will, He will. Don't you take it upon yourself to presume that He will not.

—I meant, you're very welcome.

—Now you know that's not true luv, 'adn't you better look inside the pockets of that jacket first?

—No, it's all right.

—Better look dear, your 'ubby might 'ave something tucked away in there he'd be regretting.

—No, he won't be.

—And your little girl. What lovely dresses. Are you sure? Course they do grow up so quick don't they.

But the fingers plunge as if magnetised into the pocket of the mould-coloured jacket and close round a card with metal coins on it withdraw the card it is a card of buttons four of them with heads on. The card says Christian Dior. The fingers crush the card and hide it tight.

The woman however is bending down, with pain it seems, over the open suitcase, folding the small dresses neatly one upon the other.

—What lovely dresses. This one must 'ave bin a party dress. For 'er last birthday was is luv? How old is she?

—Er . . . four, three, I mean--

—What was that luv?

—She's dead.

—Oh me darlin', me poor wee darlin'. No I won't ask how. But God isn't cruel for nothing luv, you'll see, you're young, He'll make it up to you and you still have your 'ubby who's got plenty more to give I'm sure.

—He's dead too. They were together. Yes. In an aircrash please go now.

—I will, I will. You poor wee luv. But you're young, my dear, and nice-looking as far as I can see, me eyes ain't what they used to be.

—Would you, would you like a cup of tea?

—No, luv, God bless you, you've been very good to me, but I'd better be gettin' along, I've got all the other flats to do.

—Goodbye.

—Bye luv.

—I say. Excuse me. But, what are you collecting for?

—Sorry luv?

—Where will the clothes go to?

—Oh they're for me stall. I sell them you see.

—You sell them!

—Yes, on me stall. In the market.

—Oh. I, I thought it was for some good cause. If I'd known—

—It's a good cause all right. I'm lame you know, I can't work.

—I see. Well—

—There's many poor people down my way'll be glad to 'ave them cheap. I don't make no big profit you know, by the time I've gone round all the 'ouses.

—Yes. Yes. Goodbye.

—This other case won't shut.

—I'll—let me help you.

—You're a dear, God bless you, He-will-reward-you-never-fear.

The old woman rises slowly, helping herself up with each hand on each suitcase closed. In a bent position she grasps both handles and straightens up to her short height hardly above the bent position. She waddles slowly off surrounded with the echoes of her blessings down the mottled lino towards room 32. Clearly she is held to ground-level by the double weight, for otherwise she would take off like a tiered balloon, flying along the corridor a foot or so above the mottled lino then higher, just missing the bare grey bulb that moves slightly in the draught like a small amorphous animal as she passes rooms 32, 33 and up to the vanishing perspectives of the long ceiling's edges, on out of the broken window at the other end until the door closes away the corridor the small amorphous dead animal and the vanishing perspectives, the small wide figure of the woman bending to put down her two suitcases outside room 32.

The four brass buttons on the card are almost an inch in diameter, each with a woman's helmeted head on them, Britannia perhaps or some imitation Greek goddess on the card marked Christian Dior.

The whitewood wardrobe painted pink for a girl is full of small dresses pinafores the little red wool suit the summer cotton to the right, minus the yellow one the blue velvet the crisp white frock with roses round the rim. All other things are needed the brown coat the old grey skirt the black wool dress for mourning all that came and went the pale blue cotton for summer except for the blue maternity. But more could have been given all the small dresses for example since the change of Mind and now no longer guarded by the mould-coloured jacket of the man who came and went in the wilderness.

The fourth drawer gapes open empty of baby clothes pink and white for a girl knitted socks thumb-to-fist-size clothes for two months and six twelve and eighteen sleeping and playing crying and laughing clothes. Clearly the gesture was required.

The bedclothes in the wooden cot however remain pink and white for a girl the sheets and pillow white with a pink frill the knitted blankets and the small eiderdown pink paisley patterned. And in the third drawer still the Nightdress of the Night.

The card with the four brass buttons lies uncrushed on the small pillow. I've nowhere to go says the man who came and went. Give us a bed love I won't touch you.

Everyone calls everybody love these days when there is none. Except Him whose love engulfs without uttering the word. There is no doubt, no doubt at all about that or the means provided although in His inscrutable Wisdom He changes His Mind. The time is not yet ripe He says in the month not that He has miscalculated how could He knowing all the times in one Grain of inscrutable Wisdom but that Free Will has made the ripe time now unripe. He is as disappointed as His handmaid but He knows that she will say His Will be done and bide her time and His He will return. When the time is ripe. Meanwhile He will disburden her of His Favour which He does.

But when will He return in the ripe time? The handmaid is no longer young despite the words of the little old woman shaped like a tiered balloon whose eyes aren't what they used to be. But all things are possible to the Lord even Sarah at ninety years wherefore did Sarah laugh is anything too hard for the Lord at the time appointed I will return unto thee since He hides His time for ripeness timelessly in a Grain of inscrutable Wisdom sown when He thinks fit.

The open whitewood cupboard looks bare with only half the small dresses and unguarded without the jacket of the man who came and heralded the ripeness of the time out of the wilderness and went. He says thanks old dear you're a good sort I didn't harm you did I? It'll be a ruddy miracle if you sprout a kid on that. Strange he should talk in this way. He knows. He is the Instrument. But I'll give you something to re-member me by. One day that old green jacket'll speak to you you mark my words. He opens his small suitcase and takes out a dark blue suit which he puts on over the shirt and pants he has slept in.

But now that it has spoken what is it saying?

The card with the four brass buttons lies uncrushed on the small white pillow with the pink frill. The card marked Christian Dior. Each with a woman's helmeted head.

The card was not inside the pocket on the morning of the night he came and went.

Who could have put it there? And why should He? And how, so wholly engaged in engulfing with love? But all things are possible to One who bides His time and holds space timelessly spacelessly in a Grain of inscrutable Wisdom sown as He engulfs.

The brown coat hangs next to the black wool dress two inches or three away from the small pinafores the little red wool suit the remain-ing small dresses, minus the yellow the blue velvet the crisp white frock with the roses round the rim. The coat marks the division although there are fewer adult clothes on its left than there are small clothes on its right and now the grey trousers and the mould-coloured jacket have gone as well.

The brown coat has four brown buttons of bone perhaps or plastic or-dinary suitable discreet. The card with the brass buttons lies in the palm of the left hand, the right hand fingering the embossed helmeted head. The brass buttons would certainly look brash.

But they come off the card, they are torn the card and in the drawer the zip bag made of plastic emerges zips open and emits the scissors the tin thimble the paper needle-case the black the white the pink bobbins. Black will do it does for most colours except pink and white for a girl.

The scissors cut the brown buttons from the coat. The black thread enters the needles eye. The needle sews the brass top button and the sewing occupies the silence left by the man who came and went, in and out, in and out, round the stem, stop knot and cut. And then the second button and the sewing occupies the emptiness left by the time suddenly found unripe and the disburdening of the Favour and the biding of the time to be found ripe again in and out, in and out, round the stem, stop knot and cut. And then the third, in and out. Stop knot and cut. The fourth, in the silence and the emptiness left by the sowing and unsowing of a Grain in His inscrutable Wisdom. In and out. Stop knot and cut.

The coat is wide and shapeless for a shape that came and went, with a plain high collar and the brass top button fastens at the centre. Despite the width and shapelessness the coat looks military with the brass buttons, military enough to venture out into the open world full of people and things.

The street goes down the hill or up the hill according to the viewpoint and the viewpoint faces down. The viewpoint faces down and guides the feet on down, past the Tube Station and the delicatessen with its hams and its salamis and its lachschinken, the greengrocer's slanted patchwork of apples pears tomatoes carrots cabbages, the ironmonger's with his window full of red plastic plate-racks and yellow plastic buckets nothing pink and white and pretty for a girl, the blocks of flats the bank the second-hand furniture shop with the spewing sofas and the rickety chairs and there, round the corner, is the market.

The stalls align the pavement edge, spattered with crude colour and crude coloured shouts. Fruit and vegetables, vegetables and fruit, newspaper everywhere and cabbage leaves. The next street is cleaner. Beads and costume jewellery, followed by pots and pans, followed by piled-up hats in felt and straw, followed by rolls of coloured stuffs, crude colours, followed by dresses pinafores and coats, hanging in gaudy colours over the laid-out jumpers, blouses, underwear. The woman is thin.

—Excuse-me, but do you know a short plump old lady who has a clothes stall here?

—No dear, there's so many. Three and eleven, penny change, luv. Bargains! Dresses! Cheap at the price! That one's only ten bob darlin', ten bob to you.

—She's a little deaf, and short-sighted, and lame.

—Oh, that'll be old Mrs. Turner. Short, you said, ever so little? With a big dog?

—I don't know about the dog. Where is her stall?

—What's the matter, you given 'er somat you wanna take back?

—No. No. I just wanted to see . . . her.

—She don't come Tuesdays, I don't think. She does her rounds on Tuesdays. But I could be wrong, she'd be further along, at the end of the street. Bargains! Dresses! Cheap at the price!

The street is endless with stalls and shouts that pierce the numbness round the empty hole. And people, jostling the numbness.

And there, two stalls down, is the man who came and went. In small brown check and a deerstalker unless perhaps it is a different man who never came and therefore never went. He is talking to a stall-keeper and won't turn round to show his face or the colour of his tie yellow no doubt or red.

The church is small, the mind almost as empty, though not in a mystical sense. Two pews up a woman is praying, her scarfed head bent into her hands, her body also lost in a wide-falling coat. Right up in the front pew a short fat woman sits below the Sacred Heart of Jesus revealed on a white plaster front like offal on a butcher's slab to a crowd of flickering candles below the time being indeed unripe but they don't understand. On the left the Virgin in pale cream and blue wrong again outstretches delicate unsuffering hands and smiles with vacant eyes at the unripe time and the emptiness of the small church and mind.

The brass top button is still there, between the collar bones the head embossed and helmeted, Britannia perhaps or the French one, Marianne, or an imitation goddess.

Then a great grey shaggy dog comes pattering up the aisle, its claws chicketing on the grey stone floor. The great grey shaggy dog stops here and there to sniff an empty pew, then patters on, its claws chicketing on the grey stone floor, reaches the short fat woman, and patters on, up to the altar-rail, turns left into the ladychapel, patters back and across the altar without genuflecting, pauses by the flickering candles around the odourless offal on the butcher's slab, finally vanishing to the right.

The fat woman rises, painfully it seems, blundering from the pew with two battered suitcases that hold her down to ground-level like weights on either side. Wispy grey hair sticks out from the grey woolly cap. She waddles forward to the Sacred Heart of Jesus, dumps the two suitcases invisible now behind the pew on the stone floor, bends down a little further fumbling for candles. A coin drops in the metal box.

Because life must go on.

The woman lights the candle, places it in a holder among the crowd of flickering others, straightens up to a height hardly above the bent position and stands awhile outlined against the glow.

The woman leaves the invisible suitcases before the Sacred Heart of Jesus like offerings or hostages to the offal perhaps and waddles to the right. She reappears, bent slightly forward then bends even further down to pick the suitcases, straightens and turns the corner of the pew into the aisle. She holds the great grey shaggy dog on a lead, behind her at first, then pattering past her and ahead, tugging the lead, its claws chicketing on the grey stone floor.

The woman bundles down the aisle like a tiered balloon weighted on either side. Just when the altar forms a flat frame above her head like a wide hat with flowers and a raised golden crown her eyes light up in re-cognition.

—I tied him up at the back you know. But he got loose.

—Perhaps he was in need of grace.

—What was that?

—I only said perhaps he was in need of grace.

The pale old eyes look blank, the woman nods and smiles and shuffles on.

The woman further up in the wide coat still prays, her scarfed head bent into her hands. The brass top button is still there between the collarbones. Lord as the fingers fiddle with it let the time come ripe again to the emptiness left by the disburdening of Thy Favour the sowing and unsowing the Grain of Thine inscrutable Wisdom.

Outside, the woman is still there, and her great grey shaggy dog. The man in the deerstalker and small brown check has gone.

—Excuse my waiting dear but it's so nice to see you and I'm a little 'ard of 'earing, what was it you said in there?

The grace of a dog has lost its savour in the ways inscrutable of time ripe and unripe between the sleeping waking laughing and crying clothes but not, presumably, to the woman who has not heard it.

—Only that your dog was perhaps in need of grace.

—Oh. Oh I see. Well, he 'as been a bit off-colour. He 'ad an accident you know. He was all right, nothing broken, but 'e's never bin the same since. Nasty things, accidents.

—Yes.

—Oh you poor wee darlin' what am I thinkin' of mentioning such things. You must forgive me, my memory's not what it was.

—Why . . . Oh, yes. That's all right. Are you going to your stall?

—What's that? Ooh, I say, I do like your top button.

—My top—? But they're all the same. Four of them. All the way down.

—It's gold, isn't it? I do like it. Is it a religious button?

—Well, I don't know, really. They're brass, not gold. And they're all the same.

—Oh, what a pity. You must forgive me, I can't see very well. I thought it was a religious button, with a saint on it.

—There is a head on it. It's an imitation coin.

—You're young, luv, you'll get over it. I prayed for you in there.

—It's, it's very kind of you, but . . . Are you going to your stall? May I come with you? I, please let me carry your cases.

—Oh you are good to me. I wasn't going, it's not my day you know and it's a bit late. But I will now, I will. You'll bring me luck, I feel it in me bones. It's only just down the road. Barry's more'n I can cope with I'll say.

—Barry?

—Me ole grey dog. He gets lonesome at home. So I takes him with me.

—But you didn't have him this morning?

—I did, I did. But I tied him up downstairs. Tied him up to the concrete column I did. Here we are luv, just put them there on the display, I'll unpack them.

The crisp white frock with the roses round the rim lies on top. And then the yellow one and the blue velvet. And unknown clothes belonging to room 32 perhaps or 33 or 34. She must have removed the small dresses to replace them on top, so as not to crease them. Or previous rooms flats houses the unknown clothes being underneath. Any innumerably other homes. The second suitcase disgorges anonymously also. Mauve sequins, dark brown wool. But then the blue maternity. And the mould-coloured jacket of the man who came and went.

The clothes are all laid out on the display. The crisp white frock with the roses round the rim hangs from the edge of the tarpaulin, next to the yellow one, next to the blue velvet.

—Hello, hello, hello.

The voice belongs but clangs from a night that came and went in a dark blue suit exchanged for the mould-coloured jacket left behind without the deerstalker and small brown check now here saying remember me?

—Do you want something sir, is he a friend of yours, luv, oh she's bin very good to me you know, given me such lovely things she has, the poor wee darlin'. You be kind to her, she needs a little love and comfort well, he says.

—Bargains! Lovely sparklers! Jewels! Come and see for yourself! Try it on dearie!

—What was that, luv? Why don't you go with your friend? He looks a lovely gentleman it's bad to shut yourself. You're young, m'darlin' and you've bin good to me, God-will-reward-you-never-fear.

—Well, well, here's an old friend, yes, if it isn't my old sports jacket. Down on your luck are you, I'm sorry to see that, still, I said it'd come in useful didn't I? How about a drink old girl, I owe you that.

—Mrs. Turner may I help you on your stall? Would you like some more things? I've got heaps more at home, I can go round and fetch them.

—Why, you know my name. And I don't even know yours. What was that? Well anyway you run along with your friend luv, I'll be round again, don't you worry m'darlin', you've bin very good to me and—

—God-will-reward-you-never-fear, come on old girl, I haven't got all day.

—Go away. Goodbye Mrs. Turner. I hope your dog will feel better soon.

—Oh, Barry'll be all right. He's a good dog. A bit too old, like me, and gets a bit fretful at times. But he's good company.

—Bargains! Lovely sparklers! Cheap at the price!

—Goodbye then.

—Bye-bye, luv, see you soon. And don't you fret yourself.

—Well, well, well. At last. How're you keeping, all right?

—I don't know you. Please go away.

—Oh, come on, love, you did me a good turn, you know, there's no need to get all huffy about it. I didn't harm you did I?

The fingers fiddle with the brass top button, the religious button. This was not what was wished for. Unless perhaps the inscrutable Wisdom with inscrutable instruments but no, please go away.

—All right, all right, keep your hair on. I just said I'd like to buy you a drink, that's all, for old time's sake such as it was, short and sweet you might say, but if you don't care for one fair enough. Well, so long old sport.

—Wait. I, I . . . want to ask you something.

The pub is plain, unclean, crowded with market people. The feeling is one of blankness jostled. He stands in small brown check among the drinking men, waiting for beer. Under the closed eyelids he stands half-dressed in shirt and pants by the bed saying keep your hair on I won't touch you I feel dead to the world sleep well love here, sorry I've been so long, it's market-day, there's quite a crowd as you see. Cigarette? Oh, you don't, good girl, well and how's things?

—Fine.

—Good, good. What's this you wanted to ask me then?

—Well, er, it's about the jacket, that jacket you left, did you—

—No, I don't mind your selling it love if you don't.

—I mean, inside, well, after that—

—Cheers.

—I, cheers, I became, you know . . . I mean I found—

—Bit regretful like were you dear? Stroking the empty coat? Wishing I'd given you a bit of a screw?

—Screw?

—Beg pardon. A bit of the old slap and tickle.

—?

—Lor luv a duck, when were you born?

—Nineteen—

—'eaven 'elp us, what's your name love?

—Felicity.

—Felicity! Well, Felicity-girl, d'you want me to explain how to un-screw the inscrutable as they say, at your age?

—Un . . . screw . . . ?

—Explain the facts of life to you? In my own inimitable—

—Oh. No, no. I know them. That's just what—

—Good. Good. Not that I'd have any objection mind you, though I like my women a bit smarter turned out, still, one good turn and if that's what you want well, we can do something about it, yes, why not, you're not past redemption are you, get rid of that old thing, shapeless, drab, these stalls here'll buy it from you and I'll get you a nice new costume, what d'you say to that?

—I . . . I don't understand, what do you mean, redemption, the in-scrutable, so you knew all the time, I thought so, well you'd have to wouldn't you?

—Well, used to it, women fall for me easy you know. Sorry old girl, I didn't know you were expecting it though, you know how it was, I was dead beat and you didn't exactly look, what I mean to say, yes, that's it, you looked half scared to death and, yes, that's it, I felt sorry for you, I mean, respectful like.

—Joseph.

—Jo to you. Yes, that's my name, how did you know? I guess I must have told you fancy you remembering all this time. What's yours again, oh yes, Felicity. Cor strike me dumb. I mean, nice name, Felicity. Well, Felicity-girl how about it now?

—How about, what?

—Don't play hard to get now, you're not the type, not when you're all a tingle for it, heh, how about that now, see, like it? Or this . . . ?

—I, I must go.

—Christ. A holy virgin an' all.

—Goodbye.

—Ah well.

The men jostle the numbness round the fear of the ripening time the place is full of people the door blocked the men solid immovable. The pushing of the fear across and through the male solidity reaches the door swings open full of people in the street jostling the numbness round the fear of the Lord forgive thy handmaid soiled by human touch but Thy Will Thy Will not understand the Ways of Thy time ripening refused in fear and terror of the Grain of Wisdom by inscrutable means unscrewing sowing unsowing with the Change Mind as Thou seest and the disburdening of the Favour and the biding of the time suddenly found unripe and now ripeness refused beyond redemption for Thy Way of Love to save the world by other means lost chance unless in Thy infinite Mercy Thou wilt come again as the fingers hold the brass top button tight.

The old woman stands on the threshold, so short that half the doorframe above her head is filled with the long cracked ceiling of the corridor in vanishing perspectives beyond the bare grey bulb which hangs above her head like an amorphous dead small animal in fact outside room 32, swinging a little in the draught between the vanishing perspectives of the ceiling edges. Her wispy hair sticks out of her grey woolly cap. The two suitcases on the mottled lino seem attached to her on either side, to hold her down perhaps, at ground-level, and the great grey shaggy dog looks up expectantly from the right somewhere round her waist.

—I brought Barry with me darlin'. Hope you don't mind as you've bin introduced.

—Come in, Mrs. Turner, I'm glad to see you.

—Well—

—Oh, you've got time for a cup of tea.

—You're a nice lovely girl, and a good girl, yes I will God bless you dear.

—I'll put the kettle on the ring. I've got lots of things for you. Would Barry like some water?

—What's that dear?

—Barry. Water.

—Oh, he's all right, don't you worry about him. It's ever so cosy here.

—There's not much room. But I cleared that corner, I mean I sold something that took up space and got this old table and chair down at the market and I bought a few new clothes. But please sit down.

—How you keepin' luv? Not fretting yourself?

—Here. Cups. Milk. Oh and sugar.

—And how's the nice gentleman what came to the market?

—Mrs. Turner, I have to tell you something. I'm not a widow. I mean, not the way I told you. And I never had a little girl. I thought I was going to, I bought everything in advance, I had, I had, a vision. One night. It was, oh I know what you're going to say. That's why I never told anyone. But it's true, I swear, I know it happened. Nothing could persuade me that it didn't. An angel came. Right here where you're sitting he stood, shining, shining, I felt so light. And he said I'd been chosen. It would be a girl. A woman Messiah was needed mine not to reason why but the time was right for the feminine aspect to return. And a great soft white bird descended and enfolded me. And then I felt so heavy, heavy as lead. And I grew big. Five months. Bigger and bigger. And then, well, I never fully understood it, the Favour was withdrawn. It wasn't because of my being found wanting. I did everything. But the time was not yet ripe He said and the grain grown big just vanished overnight, leaving a great big emptiness. And the means had been provided, miraculously I'd been left a little money, an old aunt you know, and I gave up my job and bought and made all the clothes, for all her ages in advance, in case it didn't last or the pound went down, the money I mean, and it didn't, the Favour was withdrawn, the time was not yet ripe. Unless, unless I dreamt it all, I came to realise the possibility, however remote, after your visit, when, but still, months, and untouched by human hand, unsoiled, but all the same, well, I must abide my time and charity begins at home other needs being greater, well, recently, only, I can't explain how after all I did get, anyway, I'd given you some of the clothes and so I sold the cot and I have lots of other things for you because after all you can't unscrew the inscrutable as they say.

The voice is low and dull. The pale old eyes look pale and old. The great grey shaggy dog patters about, its claws chicketing on the mottled lino. The great grey shaggy dog comes up and begs for a caress with an old and melancholy look and wet nose on the lap and the caress is given. The other hand covers the eyes that burn with tears at last.

—You poor wee darlin', you're still fretting yourself. You must forgive me, luv, my hearing isn't what it was and you use ever such long words. But you 'ave a good cry dear, it's good to cry, the kettle's boiling and I'll make the tea. Barry'll comfort you, now where's the teapot? Here. He's ever such an understanding dog. He knows. You'll be all right, luv, there, We'll let it brew a bit, I've given it a good stir. You'll be all right when you've 'ad a cup of tea.

The unripe emptiness has filled with words, not of communication but of love nevertheless. The priestess has both heard and not heard perhaps. The tea pours gold and clear, and then opaque into the milk. The hot tea impregnates the tightness in the throat, spreads calm into the chest and silent life. The great grey shaggy dog is still, his head caressed reposing on the knee, his old and melancholy eyes opening and closing sleepily.

—Oh, that's a lovely cup of tea, even if I say so meself. Well, I made it, but it's your tea isn't it.

—Mrs. Turner. I thought perhaps I might help you with your stall. Could I come and look after it on the days when you do your rounds? I'd like that. Not for payment, you understand.

—Yes, luv, I understand. I think it's a lovely idea.

—And I used to know people. I could ring them up, contact them again, ask them to give me clothes for you. So you wouldn't have to walk around so much.

—Don't overdo it, darlin', don't overdo it. You're a good girl all right, though, God bless you.

—I'll fetch the things I have for you. They're all ready.

The whitewood wardrobe painted pink for a girl is full of small dresses, pinafores, the little red wool suit, the summer cotton to the right, minus the yellow one, the blue velvet and the crisp white frock with roses round the rim. The brown coat to the left, the old grey skirt, the black wool dress for mourning all that came and went, the pale blue cotton for summer except for the maternity blue dress and the mould-coloured jacket of the man, the man who, well, the fourth drawer contains the baby bedclothes pink and white for a girl, the sheets and pillow white with a pink frill, the knitted blankets and the little eiderdown pink paisley patterned, and the third drawer the Nightdress of the Night.

—Here we are. We'll do it gradually. I'll give you the summer dresses later. Or perhaps you'd like some now?

—No, luv, you keep to your own time. Even the snake sheds his skins one at a time, now don't he. But you don't want to give me your coat, why, it's the coat with the lovely button, with the saint on it.

—I got myself a new one, Mrs. Turner, navy blue, much smarter. This one has done its job.

—Yes, it's the religious button, like I said, with the saint on it. Well, if you're sure, God bless you, m'darlin', it'll bring me luck, I know it will.

—Let's pack them, shall we.

—All the same, I think I'll take off them buttons, they're too good to sell. I'll put some ordinary buttons on.

—Look, I've got some brown buttons if you'd like them. The original ones. I changed them, you see. These don't really belong to the coat.

—Well, that's lovely. But you keep the religious ones, we'll cut them off if you've got some scissors have you?

—No, you take them with the coat. They'll bring you luck, you'll see.

The pale old eyes gaze silently, the woman nods.

The great grey shaggy dog patters about, its claws chicketing on the mottled lino.

—Poor Barry. He's getting a bit restless. I must be on my way. God bless you m'darlin', you're very good to me.

—See you on Tuesday then. At the market.

—That'll be nice dear.

Old Mrs. Turner rises slowly, helping herself up with each hand on each suitcase closed. In a bent position she grasps both handles, straightens up to a height hardly above the bent position and, surrounded with the silence of unspoken blessings, waddles out of the room into the hall, tugged along by the great grey shaggy dog chicketing on the mottled lino, pulling her like a bunch of untiered balloons. She nods again and moves along the corridor, weighted on either side, held down to ground-level it seems by the two suitcases, for otherwise she would surely take off along the corridor, flying a foot or so above the mottled lino towards room 32 and the bare grey bulb that swings a little in the draught like a dead small amorphous animal between the vanishing perspectives of the ceilings edges, on out of the broken window at the other end until the door closes away the corridor, the small amorphous animal, the cracked ceiling and its vanishing perspectives up above the wispy hair that sticks out of the woolly cap and little old Mrs. Turner bundled along the mottled lino by the great grey shaggy dog.

They All Go to the Mountains Now

The beach is empty as usual. All the hotels are shut and derelict and there goes Giuseppe, old before his time, his thin bony face more closely wrinkled than the sand where the sea has left it. He has aged more quickly of course, but then he always was less handsome, he would, by tacit agreement, take the plain one giorno, Giuseppe, come sta?

—O.K.—O.K., Salvatore as we used to say. What's new?

—Niente, what do you expect?

He sighs, sits down his faded denims halfway up the warm stone steps of the Byzantine church—neo-Byzantine late polychrome 11th century Lisabetta says—which casts a soothing shadow at this hour with the high rock behind it. We always sit here, facing the piazzetta and the fountain where old San Andrea carries his multiplication cross above the naked nymphs that spout water out of their mouths and some out of their full stone breasts except that they don't spout nowadays.

—They don't spout nowadays, do they, Salvatore?

—No.

Lisabetta takes a photograph of me drinking from a full stone breast, no, wait, I must get the Communist Party Headquarters in behind the Saint and the stone breasts. But the letters don't come out, the red even then faded pale pink in the hot sun and now almost invisible. And to the left of it the old shops are all shut that used to sell ceramics rubber mattresses parasols frog-flappers snorkels coloured postcards no relation to reality she says. And to the right the Pensione Central with its yellowing green shutters empty balconies all hung with bright towels and bikinis weren't they Salvatore?

—Yes.

—And we'd watch them eat their dinner up there on the terrazza in soft coloured lights. And wait for them.

To come out and offer up their bronzed bodies for further fulfilment than the sun could merely tickle up under our expert hands, below the wooden stilts of cafés built across the beach, against warm rocks or the dark wall of the stone pier out over the water, their faces rapturous in the glimmer of seafront lights under their miniskirts.

—Che dice?

—I said, some wore no pants under their miniskirts.

—Don't, Giuseppe.

—Yes, the miniskirts were good. But they didn't last, did they?

—Those were the days. The good old days.

—Our young and sexy days.

—And nights.

—Some smuggled us back to their rooms.

—The Swedish ones. Very civilised, the Swedes.

—The Germans too. More, what was the word, Salvatore?

—Gemutlice.

—The English were the easiest, though.

—Don't say that, Giuseppe.

—And the least supple and the most badly dressed.

—That's not altogether true, Giuseppe, there are always exceptions. What would you say if an Englishman came along, or a German for that matter, and declared that all Italian women stink of sweat and garlic?

—I'm sorry, Salvatore, I forgot.

—That's all right, Giuseppe. It was nothing really.

—I know.

—It was different in the old days.

—Our young and sexy days.

—Our young and sexy days.

—Yes.

—You look tired, Giuseppe, your eyes have lost their youthful passion.

—So have yours, Salvatore.

—Me? What are you saying, Giuseppe? Why, only last week a lady tourist told me there was passion in my eyes, a smouldering passion, she said.

—Well, there isn't much choice nowadays, Salvatore. The young men have all left, and the tourists don't come any more. She must have been at least forty-five.

—But ravenous.

—You mean she tired you out?

—How can you say such a thing?

—Well, you look a little flabby these days, Salvatore.

—I still have remnants of vital flesh around me.

—In folds.

—Just because you're skinny and wrinkled.

—She didn't seem to mind about empty beaches and the big scare, did she? I suppose she was past caring. Did she really tire you out, Salvatore?

—Well, sometimes the ripe ones are pretty terrific you know. But of course she wasn't as luscious as, you know, what we've been used to.

—No.

She wasn't as luscious as the young bronzed bodies with the small firm white breasts and the thin white line across the triangle of fur and across the buttocks where the bikinis had protected them from the once invigorating rays like minipants and bras made of white skin alone on the white sheets or else standing below the wooden stilts of cafés built over the beach, against warm rocks or the dark wall of the stone pier where some wore nothing under their short skirts in sheer anxiety for those swift fingers that caress and open up the folds of oh Giuseppe's hand inside his pocket in between his legs follows the same thoughts though his eyes without a smouldering passion gaze vacantly at the dry stone breasts that surround San Andrea bent under his multiplying cross. Poor Giuseppe. His thin bony face is more closely wrinkled than the sand where the sea has left it. But he always was less handsome, the follower in our operations as we surveyed the field, numbering the possibilities in order of attraction, danger, likelihood, nationality, for these things matched in relatively few permutations except once when danger came surprising overwhelming.

Poor Giuseppe. It is a tacit agreement between us that he takes the plain one.

They always come in twos. For company. But speak little to each other as they lie white and vulnerable on their bright towels and under no umbrella, unaware of the first day's vivid pink they turn. Che bella! is the most we venture as we saunter our dark brown bodies indolently by for their covert inspection behind our muscled backs. The routine is the same. We let them get over the sunstroke first, a day or more, in bed but useless, unless by chance the pretty one is less susceptible to sunstroke and comes out alone, but that's not so good as she feels obliged to wear indignant virtue then. In twos it looks all right, just sociable, getting to know the natives. The plain one uses the pretty one as bait, the pretty one uses the plain one to keep up the appearances.

It is astonishing how long one can communicate with so few words. Hot. Coca-cola? O.K.? Die Sonne ist warm. Schwimm? Nein. Gut. Bella. Sol. Aqua. Si. And fingers running sand on to a thigh or cleavage perhaps according to encouragement then brushing it off with laughter. Sometimes one of the town's inept can be watched as he plonks himself down by a couple of pale Irish girls or the like and lamely tries his luck into long silences when they don't know how to say go away you cheeky thing and don't know whether they want to just in case nothing better turns up, they're easy enough words to learn after all, and stare into the distance sitting up playing with sand missing their full share of the sun rather than lie back helpless and seductive until at last he goes away thinking how dull they are. It is an art to make even the stupidest conversation seem picturesque novelty, the indispensable ingredients being sexual excitement and hope of true romance raised between the words and gestures. Giuseppe can't do it on his own. He and the plain one are the reflectors of our generative current, bask in our gaiety, imitate and echo. But that too is exciting, like a grotesque mirror.

And the two friends who chose each other for company but hardly spoke come alive scream with laughter play ball, hunt shells and coloured pebbles leap into the sea dance to the local groups make love below the wooden stilts of cafés built over the beach, against the warm rocks or the dark wall of the stone pier, their sunbrown faces rapturous in the glimmer of lights from the seafront. The town is full of bronze couplings, in every room and corner what with the pick-ups and the honeymooners. Only the married ones, clearly, the next day, have not.

They come in twos, they go, they come. We learn to make distinctions at a glance, the typists waitresses telephonists with little poise in court-ship, the hairdressers and elegant shopgirls with much, the students who think themselves superior and don't know how to cope. Some you can pinch the bottom of chuck the chin of and tell them you'll come to me tonight almost as a first sentence. For others you have to lay out a show of gallantry, always within the act of local poverty however since most will pay for drinks and dancing offer cigarettes and generally de-mand nothing except our skilful hands all over their bronzed bodies un-der the stars in the warm night to the sound of the sea and soft Italian words of love Lisabetta te amo.

Lisa. Lisabetta. She comes alone. Suntanned already from some other place, Positano, Sorrento, ruined she says much too crowded and pebbles just like here apart from tiny coves, I prefer a sandy beach es-pecially all wrinkled where the sea has left it, but at least here it's quieter, less pretentious. Quieter? It doesn't seem quiet to me. That's because you don't know other beaches, I'll take you. She speaks fluent Italian with odd bits of Spanish, so alike I get them mixed up, the little words especially, you know, the auxiliaries. Whatever those may be. She tosses her long blonde straight thick hair at the local inept who clum-sily plonk themselves down by her to try their luck and tells them to bugger off. I chose you from the first day she says, but you were busy with that plump Finnish girl what a waste so I waited. How did you know she was Finnish? I heard her speak near-perfect English with a Swedish lilt and she looks Hungarian, that's how. I chose you from the start, you're the most handsome and intelligent looking, why did you take so long? I didn't dare, you frightened me. Yes, I'm good at that, it works better in the end. Doesn't it, Salvatore, caro mio, doesn't it with her long blonde straight thick hair over my face chest thighs doesn't it?

She still frightens me. She drives a small white Spitfire convertible with two black leather seats very fast along the coast bends to Salerno or up the *autostrada del sol* to Napoli or down to Paestum and its long wild sandy beach where you can almost see Aphrodite stepping from the waves I mean Venus, she says, you know, the goddess of love and beauty. Look at the wrinkles on the sand there where the sea has left it and she explains the ruined temples in the sun the megalithic dolmens the remains of Pompei the museum the churches frescoes carvings sculptures in strange places which I didn't know we had and our own church neo-Byzantine, Salvatore, she says, late polychrome 11th century and can't you see these paintings underneath the colonnade were done in the nineteen thirties? Or twenties at the earliest. Pity, and she shows me why in detail that I don't remember but I duly find them truly ugly at once which before I was proud of. She's writing a book and she knows everything but clear and simple she makes it, not like culture at all, opening up worlds of terror that all this beauty exists like her love and will vanish for ever. She stretches my horizons like elastic and to breaking point or else they will shrink back into short shrift from silly little girls and swift snatched sex and solitude after the mating season.

But even the tourists acquire new angles in her amused comments as she translates what the Germans say, the French, the English, the Americans. Chasse gardée, she says a middle-aged man from the Midlands who stands in his misshapen trunks among a group of bored and cream-white girls who will certainly get sunstroke and don't know how to get rid of him as he utters long slow platitudes endlessly, smoking a big cigar. A village explainer, she says. That's what Einstein said about Ezra Pound, you know, a village explainer, which is fine, if you're a village. Who was Einstein, you mean the man who invented the atom bomb? No, Salvatore, he didn't, and I didn't say Einstein, I said Gertrude Stein. Oh, a woman. Well? And do you know who Ezra Pound was? Yes, a Fascista. A poet, Salvatore, a poet, that's all that will matter in a hundred years' time. Do you worry about the politics of those who made Pompei or Paestum or even these horrible paintings on your church here? No, but then I don't worry about those people anyway they're all dead and life's too short to know so much you make me feel Sal-va-to-o-o-o-re!

—There's your Marisa calling you.

—Oh, to hell with her.

—Don't say that, Salvatore, you know you'll be all sweet to her again this winter, after September even, when the season is over.

—Lisabetta. Marry me.

—She'll make you a good wife, Salvatore, she loves you, she'll be faithful, she'll bear you lots of bambini and she's pretty, too. What more do you want?

It's all because of my poverty, that's what it is, they're all the same, already on the second day she was asking what I did, and wouldn't believe me you, a student? on holiday? and what are you studying, which university, ah, mechanical engineering, so, which college, what branch, how far have you got and with technical details I can't even remember now three weeks later so that in the end I admit to transporting empty bottles in a small three-wheeler from the hotels at dawn, not too well-paid but who wants to be a waiter at sixteen hours a day and never a moment for . . .

—Prowling.

—Yes. But I love you Lisa.

—And what will it lead to, Salvatore?

—I don't know, oh, I know I'm not up to, I mean, well, but I just love you.

—I meant, the transporting of empty bottles in a small three-wheeler at dawn? Haven't you any ambition?

I have ambition to hold her in my arms, her body and her thick long straight blonde hair and the worlds of terror that all this beauty exists like her love and will vanish for ever staying technically virgin till marriage.

—Che dice?

—The American girls, Salvatore, don't you remember, they'd allow everything but. Disgusting I call it.

—Oh, shut up, Giuseppe. Why do we have to have this stupid conversation day after day?

—Ah. I see your mind is on higher things.

—You're pathetic, that's what you are. A dirty old man.

—We're the same age, Salvatore.

—You understand nothing.

—Well, it's not just age, Salvatore, we could cope with that if things were going on around us, we could watch at least, but now, there's nothing, all the young men gone, the hotels shut, and nobody coming.

—Yes, all right, all right.

—It was different in the old days ... Our young and sexy days.

—Our young and sexy days!

—Before that crazy doctor found the cancer in the sun.

—Not in the sun, stupid.

—I mean in the skin under the sun, Salvatore, of course.

—A can-cer-i-ge-nous virus, responding to certain ra-di-ation le-vels in the rays, together with the ra-diation in the sea since the underwater tests, affects the o-zone, which is oxy-gen three, that is, oxy-gen with three atoms instead of two, an un-stable e-le-ment ...

—Yes, I know, you read it up in the paper, I remember the day. But it was already too late when you read it. Everyone had stopped coming. Amazing how quickly news travels. Or perhaps they saw it on television before we did. It all happened so suddenly.

—No it didn't, Giuseppe, it merely seemed to. People talked about it at first, but you never listen. And then one year there were fewer, I mean, rooms could occasionally be found, even in August, don't you remember those French girls who came without reservations? That was unheard of before. And then the following year, rooms could be found quite easily. And then—

—And then nothing.

—Not that it would have made much difference to us, Giuseppe, we were getting on, married and settled down—

—So that paper you read, it was only a posto ... posto ...

—Postmortem, Giuseppe.

—Yes ... Perhaps they're all dead.

—No they're not.

—You mean ... you still hear, Salvatore?

—Once a year. On my son's birthday. She sends me a photograph. Poste restante.

—Postmortem? Why?

—Poste restante, Giuseppe, it means I collect it at the post office. I have seventeen. She brought him up all by herself. She called him Kevin, I can't think why but I know he's mine. He's beautiful, Giuseppe.

—And she never bothered you at all?

—Il mio bambino inglese. He's beautiful. I keep them hidden in a box in a hole in a secret cave. I can't tell you where. I've never told anyone this much, Giuseppe.

—Che amico mio.

His eyes that have lost the passion of our young and sexy days briefly regain the old grateful look of a faithful dog, follower in all our operations as we surveyed the field, then turn away simultaneously with mine towards the old Santo bent under his multiplying cross above the full stone breasts that spout nothing at all, his bony face more closely wrinkled than the sand where the sea has left it.

—Salva-to-o-o-o-re!

—There's your Marisa calling you.

—Ah yes. Well, I'd better go.

—Ciao, Salvatore, see you.

—Ciao, Giuseppe.

—Salvatore.

—Yes?

—There's just one thing I've never understood.

—Che cosa?

—Well, if the sun and the sea's so dangerous now, why don't we die of it? All that, what was it, that gets into our skin—

—Ozone.

—Yes, well, we get it all day, that cancer. Why are we alive?

—We're born with it, Giuseppe, immune, I mean, you know, like vaccination.

—I see.

—Well, ciao.

—And why don't they collect it up, in seaweed for instance, and vaccinate everybody?

—Perhaps they will, Giuseppe. I expect they're working on it now.

—And then everyone will come back?

—Well, we'll be old by then.

—Yes. We'll be old.

—Sal-va-to-o-o-o-re!

—In the meantime, well, they all go to the mountains now.

—The good old days have gone.

—Our young and sexy days as you would say Giuseppe.

—Yes.

—Well, ciao.

—Ciao Salvatore. See you tomorrow.

Medium Loser and Small Winner

Henry the Navigator the Infanta sails all night, watching himself inside the murmuring calculations of total emptiness.

She says. She tends to say such things, that demand a pinprick or at least a deflationary stare and query like who's he or wouldn't Christopher Columbus be more appropriate?

—Columbus had three ships. Crank insists on only one.

—You're very sure of yourself, aren't you?

—No. Columbus succeeded. Henry the Navigator sailed into disaster.

—So? Tragedy as well.

—You stole his wife.

—My dear, stole is hardly the word.

—'Don't dramatise!'

—You're the one—

—That's what I mean. I spoke in quotes.

—Ah. You should signalise them in your tone of voice.

—I did. And the exclamation mark. But you never hear my modulations.

—I hear them in bed. At least the exclamation marks. I imagine that there you don't feel obliged to speak in quotes.

—I think that I preferred it abstract.

She murmurs. Or so I think I hear for she has murmured the phrase before, unheard or half-heard perhaps in hotel rooms and heard now for the first time or reconstructed retrospectively. Nothing deserves a rush of preference. No, nor woman neither.

Quinta-la-blonde-aux-blanches-mains makes emotional scenes, disguising them as philosophic queries that both repel and hold the involvement as her sudden intensity creates magnetic fields on the spindle-legged table between us in the espresso bar or is it the white-clothed table in the Soho restaurant. You know what I mean, staring at her elegant hands and their long nails varnished in silver pink. If only, well, at least, the little that exists of it . . .

Go gently now.

—The little that exists of it exists.

—You don't give many signs of it.

—Signs?

—Little things. An occasional expression of appreciation. You know, a slight term of endearment. Why, you don't even use my name. Quinta! Where did you get hold of that?

—I told you.

—It has nothing to do with me. I mean, it doesn't even suit me. You give the impression that you think nothing, nothing of me at all.

—I shall always think, I always think, warmly of you.

I suppose, says Quinta-la-brune, whose short dark hair stars the pillow next to mine in the hotel room, I felt the challenge of your unreflecting ways. She has small strong brown hands and sensual fingers, which nervously smooth the crumpled sheets.

Why try to bring back in a weary sigh the initial dazzle, the mild curiosity that grows slowly obsessive with the luxury of drift into another being who stands alone in the crowded reception room sky-scraped high above London and full of mathematicians and nuclear or is it electronics engineers in hopeful get-together with heavy industry. She wears no lipstick only kohl around her long light eyes that look through me for someone. The massive sandy hair piled up in shells above her neck has lighter strands of early grey perhaps but surely not. She looks through me for someone, fragile in sleeveless pink against the groups that modulate in close attempts not to meet one another, their left hands holding wine glasses and right hands holding snippets or vice versa in the crowded room. A tall thin man walks up to her out of the mathematical units grouped and wraps her with attention, touches her elbow as a means of steering her towards the table full of drinks and snippets. Childish excitement transforms her small face and despite the massive sandy hair with lighter strands of perhaps early grey she looks about fourteen. She envelops her words with gestures, rounded ones, linear ones, angular nervous ones, she doesn't shave under the arms and eats no snippets but accepts a cigarette and a glass of white wine so that the gestures stop. She wears no lipstick only kohl around the long green eyes that look past the thin man for someone.

The speeches have begun. The carpeted room absorbs them and everyone goes on talking. A red-faced man in tails and white tie bangs a gong next to the microphone, producing a brief moment of silence which ceases in the space between the gong and the units of manhood that surround her. She carries no bag, no glass, no cigarette and shapes her words with gestures of a smooth circular kind, or rectilinear, nervous and emphatic, pushing the air between us until I feel faint with absorbing her strained enthusiasms or with not eating snippets. Her eyes look past the men for someone, straight at Brazilian Felix who comes up to join the group with a glass of wine in each hand one for her. She smiles and takes a sip. Her kohl-edged eyes look over the transparent rim at Felix.

Now that the moment has come I hesitate, drained by the redirection of her pale energy which now no longer functions in the air between us as she sips her wine and looks meaningfully at Felix or listens merely or talks quietly without gestures, on account of the heat perhaps. The illusion of heat, because the sky-scraped picture windows give a cold still of London grey under grey clouds. But the electronics and the mathematical units generate heat and noise between us which I wade through to reach her sleeveless pink that shows the blonde unshaven armpits when she clothes her words in gestures weaving a spell over Felix, old chap.

Mrs. he introduces and she smiles into my blatant interest. So you are one of the mysterious heavy industrialists?

—Heavy we may be, but mysterious no, it's the mathematicians who are mysterious, wouldn't you say? Or are you one yourself?

—Me? Utterly brainless, can't you see? No, my husband, Christopher is. Crank, she says introducing him, come meet a giant industrialist who's decided at last to eat up mathematicians instead of time-and-motion experts. She looks into my blatant interest as if to say I eat men too. And how will you take to this change of diet?

—A few ideals never hurt anyone, says Crank, but as I prepare a genial no-indeed-not she breaks into soft high mirth and wifely echoing knowledge that he means ideal numbers, that is, dividers of prime numbers whereas by definition prime numbers have no dividers but themselves and unity. You see? As if to say I learn something from all my men. I lag behind, she says straight into my blatant interest, he wades through equations to reach me but I don't really exist. You know, like a straight isotrope.

—Darling you know very well that the straight isotrope is one of the most beautiful discoveries of mathematics.

—Only one?

They seem to have gone through this routine many a time which says availability providing you can fight at his own game with his own transfinite numbers the guardian of her nonexistent straightness. I never got beyond Pythagoras myself and the square on the hypotenuse at present is clearly Brazilian Felix taut short intense but a big business man who knows his business although her green eyes dip into my blatant interest and size up my heavy industriousness large affability and confidence that ask how straight right into hers would a straight isotrope be?

—I lag behind, I told you. I merely pick the things he says and wear them at parties by way of decoration, like jewels you know. But I lose them quickly.

—A beautiful woman doesn't need—

—If you must pay me compliments please try to think up original ones, Mr. what was your name again?

—Basil.

—Basil. Hmmm. Basil-the-boss. You have a long large office carpeted in purple with creamy wild silk curtains, a curved ivory-coloured desk and purple telephones and empty in and out trays. Your secretary is svelte and elegant and in love with you but you are faithful to your splendid, generously proportioned wife who knows no sorrows of the flesh, which sorrows attend only the fleshless, and she is called, let me see, yes, Daphne.

—Do you always invent stories about people you don't know?

—Sometimes. Some people aren't worth inventing stories about.

—And do they come true?

—As true as a straight isotrope.

—And how straight is a straight isotrope?

Her eyes have sized me up, measured me as a heavy industrialist in the back of Christopher who talks to Felix fully aware of shifting polygons. Her hand holding the glass is white and elegant with long nails varnished silver pink. Since it doesn't exist she says with sudden intensity that promises much in bed, I imagine it can be taken as straight or as unstraight as you wish to make it, and the verbs rouse my masculine prerogative to a sudden steady now, nothing deserves a rush of preference. So you play games with words? Dangerous games.

—No, I don't like games. I always lose them. But then, I tend to lose things.

—Things?

—Oh, boring things, like the sex-war and all that, if it exists. By saying it now, you see, I've lost it already. Tell me, Basil-the-boss, you don't need a secretary by any chance, or would someone else, she adds quickly, somewhere in your outfit? I'm looking for a job.

—Ah, Phoebe my dear. I want you to meet may I call you Quinta? This is Phoebe, my wife.

—How do you do.

But she looks surprised, not at my splendid wife, amply proportioned in a childlike innocence quite unmarred by all that flesh and the sorrows thereof, which sorrows attend only the fleshless unlike me, but at the name I call her. Do you always tag names on people, she murmurs, that from you with the stories you attach to names, *touché* she says and *touché* it is. Christopher, come meet Basil and Phoebe and he turns from Felix fully aware of shifting polygons. Actually everyone calls him Crank. You must both come and see us.

Her green eyes stare into my rush of preference as she stretches out a long white hand in farewell full of the naked vulnerability she has let me glimpse between the frilly display of enthusiasm for words and things. The hand presses on Felix's arm with more than fond farewell under the varnished silver pink.

Crank has no fondness however for quadratic equations and so dutifully she keeps quite separate her ideal numbers that divide prime numbers which by definition have no dividers but themselves and unity. Separate, she insists, with wifely echoing knowledge, from the full life of transfinite numbers she leads with Crank. And do you call all your mistresses Quinta? she rings me at the office which has no purple carpet but pearly thermoplastic tiles and rectangular teak desk with merely ivory and steel-blue telephones, a picture-window sky-scraped high over London beyond white-slanted blinds the whole thing pure, frigid and clinical or is it some hotel, cocktail bar, restaurant, pub, the dialogue scattered over various places times agglomerating only in retrospect. You are the fifth, that's all. Not too reprehensible for a man of fifty. My great love I add quickly.

—Quinta-la-blonde, she murmurs. And what of Quinta-la-brune? Quinta-la-rousse?

—What of them?

—Quinta-la-brune had short hair, starring the pillow. She made emotional scenes, disguising them as philosophic queries, ruining your vague content with her black sails, conjured on far horizons. She said I suppose I felt the challenge of your unreflecting ways.

—Did she?

—And do you really love me? And you said of course I love you, haven't I shown? And she said well, but you don't give many signs of it. Signs? You said. Little things, she said. It's the little things that count. An occasional expression of personal endearment for instance. You seem to take me completely for granted. So of course you had to get rid of her.

—Of course.

—You don't even call me by my name, she said.

—Well, what do you expect, her name was . . . let me see, Beatrice.

—I must say I preferred it abstract.

—So you still invent stories about people you don't know, people who don't exist?

—If they are worth a story, they exist.

—And I suppose you still insist on calling me Basil-the-boss?

—No. I can call you Felix if you like.

—I don't like.

—I have a cousin called Felix who used to bully me and grew into a small sad man.

—Thank you.

—Well but you see you will change the image. He always has some calamity to tell. I said to him once, one day Felix, you will tell me a happy story. I haven't seen him since.

—You've seen our mutual Brazilian friend though.

—Felicio? Yes, I've seen him. He worships me. With an intensity I didn't know still hit people.

—And it bores you?

—No. I lap it up. It makes for instant communication at all levels.

—Oh, so you've got that far?

—Really! You have the crudest mind.

—Well, you said all levels.

—I mean, he basks in all my enthusiasms—

—For ideal numbers.

—But he has none himself, except for me. Oh, and literature.

—So you prefer my unreflecting ways.

—I don't know.

—And Crank?

—I don't know.

She suddenly looks crumpled and about fourteen. He wades through equations to reach me, say her sea-green eyes, sailing all night, watching himself inside the murmuring calculations of total emptiness. I only want, she says self-pity in her voice, a little tenderness. She only wants, I know, a man who can make her come.

And so she sits in coffee-bars with Felix and her enthusiasm for ideal numbers, words and things. No one deserves a rush of preference, however, and so she sits with Felix or lies who knows, while Crank wades through equations to reach her and splendid Phoebe full of fleshy understanding for my rushes and the emptiness they bring enfolds me as our comfortable bodies love in the old familiar places. You catch them on the rebound, she says, over a broken marriage, after a nervous breakdown, during a bad patch. No need for too much effort in seduction then. Only a small persistence at first perhaps.

Yet the persistence however small persists. The electronic circumstance or the straight isotrope or even a piqued sense of failure needling the rush of preference. Happy? Ahum. The slight nod, the half-lie express some sort of truth and she sits quite still, or is it stubbing out her cigarette nervously under long nails varnished in silver pink, her vulnerability almost tangible.

Quinta-la-blonde-aux-blanches-mains turns and looks sidelong at me then across the restaurant to the back of a man's head just visible over a wood partition, a rectangular greying head that aches a tensity between them as recognition surely lurches in her veins or mine.

—My first lover, she says casually, conjuring arithmetical progression.

—You pedant, she says then, first just means none before, there must occur a first. Women's love isn't arithmetical, like men's. First means first last and only, she adds, dark with scorn, any other means no more than identifying, failing and getting hurt, as you have hurt me, and it hurts just a little as she stares straight at the back of the head above the wood partition. But the law of probability brings infinitesimals into the space between as the man turns his receding brow, flattened nose, thin wide mouth along the dropped tension in her veins or mine and proclaims a different man, a different species altogether outside the radius of that love or this.

—There now occurs a pseudo-conversation.

—And what might you mean by that?

—You know, the kind of conversation we have in order to avoid the other kind, which goes like this.

—Like what?

—I mean, since you're taking the afternoon off, shall we stay here and have another drink till it's time for the film or shall we drive out into the country?

—I don't mind.

—Well, which do you prefer?

—I have no preference. It's pleasant here.

—But it's a lovely day for the country.

—All right, let's go.

—No, you said you wanted to stay here.

—I didn't. I only meant, whichever you like.

—You didn't, you know.

—All right I didn't. Let's go.

—We'll stay here.

—For heaven's sake, stop fussing. What do you want?

—Just, that you should express a preference.

—I don't care. I said I'd—

—You don't care about anything, do you?

—There you go again, generalising from the particular.

—For once you had a tiny enthusiasm. You wanted, you actually wanted to stay here and have another drink, and perhaps see the film, though you didn't say so, rather than—

—You and your enthusiasms.

—You see, that's how it goes. Well, we'd better have the pseudo-conversation.

—So you've started labelling conversations now?

—They tell a story.

—Hmmm. Yes, you like inventing stories, don't you? You even invent them about me.

—Not now. But I did, before I met you.

—Oh? I hope I came up to expectations.

—A story doesn't have expectations.

—What does it have then? Transfinite numbers? Tell me, I like to learn too.

—A banal story doesn't bear the telling.

—I see. Well I hope I didn't come up to the no expectations.

—Or the living either. But you had no name. Only a sort of label.

—Dangerous things, labels.

—Just a game. You once said I played dangerous games. But sometimes labels turn out, later, to speak the truth.

—You tend to lose games, you said.

—Thank you for remembering something about me.

—I remember several things about you.

—Full stop. Start again. Do you like Machado de Assis?

—Never heard of it.

—He wrote *Epitaph of a Small Winner*. Or so it's called in English. In
Portuguese it's *Memorias postumas de Bras Cubas*.

—Oh.

—I suppose you prefer automation reports?

—Well, yes, if you insist.

—You do? Tell me why.

—I just do. Stop analysing. As if I could share with her my enthusiasm
for computers that screen industrial designs in three dimensions.

—'You have romantic tastes, hidden under all that massive lack of ex-
uberance.'

—There you go again, with your generalisations.

—I spoke in joking quotes. You told me to stop analysing.

—Your verbal anarchy dazzles me my dear. When you're not misusing
Crank's mathematical language you echo Felix's native enthusiasms and
spill them all over me. Why should I care about some latest author in a
language neither of us reads?

—Actually, Machado de Assis died a hundred years ago.

—May his soul rest in peace.

—Full stop. Start again.

—No I won't. If you can't talk normally I'd rather stop.

—Yes, let's stop.

I just find, she says after a while self-pity in her voice, your lack of enthusiasm for things so hard to bear.

—Quinta my dear. That's not true. I just don't rush.

—You rushed for me.

—I mean I don't invent things to enthuse about.

—But I don't either. They're there. Even the people I invent stories about. They all exist. It makes life more exciting.

—I also see the daisies on the way.

—But I see daisies too. Only, only I prefer sunflowers.

—I like sunflowers too.

—You don't. Whenever I mention a sunflower you shrug and say it leaves you cold or you've never heard of it.

—Mention a sunflower.

—Well . . . instant, communication, at all, levels for example.

—Instant communication at all levels, to me, means what it says.

—It says what it says. It does not say what it does not say.

—The Sibyl hath uttered.

—You think so ill of me. What have I done that you should pick on me like that, accusing me—for instance—of arithmetical progression in love.

—You used the phrase, your first lover. I merely said it conjures arithmetical progression. I spoke in joking quotes.

—Do you love me . . . a little?

—In my own no doubt lethargic way I probably love you more than you love me. You love only yourself. And your enthusiasms' and stories about people which express only yourself.

—A hit, a palpable hit. Quick, don't let go, a real conversation, why, you've actually expressed an opinion.

—You child. I would call that a pseudo-conversation.

She sighs and murmurs half-inaudibly, yes, I must say that I preferred it abstract.

—And I must say that if you must say things like that as a mathematician's wife you should define your terms.

—Why? I must stop generalising, analysing, labelling, inventing stories, I must define my terms. But you generalise and label all the time.

What is Quinta but a label you've given me, and without defining the term? You only dislike nails on the head when they hurt something in you.

—Try . . . not hurting.

—Sooner or later, however, it materialises. The descent into the physical occurs, and with the physical, words, words, he wades through words to reach—

—Who wades?

—What? Oh, nothing. No one. And then we have a pseudo-conversation to avoid the other kind which goes like this. Like what? Like shall we go to the cinema or to bed? At least you will express a preference there, I know.

But afterwards she cries out into the pillow her ideal numbers perhaps, that divide prime numbers which by definition have no dividers but themselves and unity, unless it be the straightness of a non-existent isotrope or else quite simple bathos such as leave me, Crank, leave me, I don't deserve you or anyone else, so that inevitably I tend to balance out the accounts, the equations she would say or shift the polygons with a visiting Irrigation Engineer from Brazil, an antique goddess proportionate to her country, fifty-five if a day with fluffed-up dyed black hair and bulging eyes and an enormous mouth who makes a dead set for me at some reception or other. You, an Irrigation Engineer? Shto whisky me mata, and she clucks with laughter, and tumbles nice in bed, maish, maish, she clucks and coos like a motherly hen, boa, boa, maish, maish, but this to flatter me for in fact she satisfies easy and shows me just what does more than some women will in all that flesh and the sorrows thereof, which sorrows seem to attend only the fleshless, maish, that engulfs, presumably the Irrigation Engineer. She sleeps now with her enormous mouth wide open in the filtered light from the hotel's nylon curtains and her neck all round in folds and the sheets below in wrinkles. Adeush, adeush, carinho, e muite obrigado. She has no name or number unlike splendid Phoebe full of fleshly understanding for my rushes and the occasional plenitude they bring who enfolds me as our comfortable bodies love in the old familiar places—

At the far corner table across the crowded dining room the small man holds his chin in his left thumb and taps the left side of his nose repeatedly with his left forefinger, every day between courses, sometimes however the right side of his nose with his right forefinger, according perhaps to which side his young swarthy wife sits. Felix I call him in my mind's melancholy eye, after a cousin who chieftained all the games we played but grew up small and sad, and never smiles, and tells calamities to all who ask him how he is. One day, Felix, you will tell me a happy story. I haven't seen much of Felix lately.

Felix, who probably bears the name of Joaquím, or João, or even perhaps Julho de Janeiro, stares miserably across the dining room full of French, German, English, Portuguese, and taps the left side of his nose repeatedly with his left forefinger. His wife talks in an animated way to Phoebe at the next table, at least I call her that for she reminds me of Phoebe, splendid type Crank teases my thinness with, amply proportioned in a childlike innocence quite unmarred by all that flesh and the sorrows thereof, which sorrows seem to attend only the fleshless. Teased, I should say, for Crank has left me.

Felix, who probably bears the name of João, or even Julho de Janeiro looks glum and taps his nose. His wife talks in an animated way to Phoebe, and perhaps also to Phoebe's dark thin husband who has his back to the dining room full of French and so on. I sympathise, for I wear sunglasses at meals to hide the fact that I shed tears at times up in my cubic bedroom despite the window on the sky the sea the golden rocks from which the agaves spike.

If Felix had two wives sitting on either side he would hold his chin in both his thumbs and tap both sides of his nose with both his forefingers. Or his wife and his mother, expected down tomorrow perhaps, his wife befriending fat Phoebe and her dark thin husband to align the alliances in advance.

—Do you always invent stories about people you will never see again? Basil-the-boss demands in the reception room that sky-scrapes the London sky or in the little Soho restaurant or where I can't remember.

—Oh yes, and I stick names on people.

—And how do you know the names belong?

—It doesn't matter does it?

—One day you will tell me a happy story.

I sympathise, for I wear dark glasses to hide the fact that Crank has left me at last, for chronic cannibalism. I eat men. Not all the time of course, every few years or so it comes over me. Or rather, let the truth burn like the Algarve sun, I nibble at them, and they nibble at me, and then, before I can say lo and farewell, they have eaten me, the mediummen, and spewn me forth like ectoplasm. I wouldn't mind so much your eating them, says Crank, but I do object to letting them eat you. It makes you like like ectoplasm.

But the Algarve sun tans me deep gold and my unvarnished nails grow long and white. My cousin Felix bullied me as bullies Fátima on the sand behind their mothers' bulging naked backs, attacking her with all his might and a yellow wooden spade.

—Lolita! nasals out a bulging back. Laolita! Venhapraquí! Venhapraquí!

But Lolita vengs not.

The sea murmurs maternally beyond the cackle. João attacks Fátima with all his might and a yellow wooden spade. Fátima towers two inches over him, toddles away and plonks herself in blithe indifference or suddenly overcome. Creeps up behind her and crowns her head with a bucketful of sand. Fátima yells. The mothers cluck and spank and cries into fat naked thighs, Fátima sobs into fat naked arms and all pain has equality in its nakedness but passes in a flash as Fátima burbles happily with her bucket and pushes his blue plastic boat along the sand to make a winding track which he destroys under his following knees as he creeps up from behind and attacks Fátima with all his might and his blue plastic boat. Fátima yells, repeat performance.

—Lolita!

But Lolita vengs not.

João surely grows up into a small sad man who sits at the corner table across the dining room holding his chin in his left thumb and tapping the left side of his nose repeatedly with his forefinger, every day between courses, but today he holds his chin in both thumbs and he taps both sides of his nose with both his forefingers. His swarthy wife talks in an animated way to splendid Phoebe and perhaps to Phoebe's dark thin husband who has his back to the dining room. On Felix's right at the same table the grey-haired woman sits in black, with Felix's long nose and sad brown eyes, and talks to Felix earnestly as he taps his nose on both sides with both his forefingers.

—One day you will tell me a happy story, says Basil-the-boss in the espresso bar, the hotel room, the Rover 2000.

—One day, Basil-the-boss, one day I will.

—One day you'll stop calling me that I hope. Do you always stick labels on people?

—Sometimes labels speak the truth.

The French still talk of routes. I generalise from many particulars right here. Good roads, bad roads obsess them, especially, it seems, la route de Saragosse.

—Flugzeug, says the baby-faced German, curtly refusing to discuss the roads and I sympathise, for I wear dark glasses to hide the fact that I shed tears at times up in my cubic room despite the view and the Three Fates, for example, who walk on the dusty road in the heat of noon, dressed all in black with black scarves on their heads, sharing a black umbrella.

—Space stretches time, says the thinnest of the three, presumably in local dialect, it translates time into locality.

—The sun burns, says the fattest, pass me the umbrella.

—I carry the umbrella, says the tallest, you'll only knock it into my blind eye.

—She cheats, though, says the thinnest and most angular, with a descent from space into new matter.

—The sun burns everywhere, says the fattest and most panting. She won't escape.

—Not everywhere, says the tallest and most knowing. I carry the um-brella and can see further than you, despite my blind eye.

Nobody talks like that. Nobody talks the way I want them to. Nobody thinks the way I think they think. I sometimes try to imagine myself a medium-man who nibbles at me with the selfish carelessness I find so challenging until I suddenly look like ectoplasm, says Crank who loves me, whom I love and hurt, you fawn on those who don't give a damn, why can't you concentrate on me for a change. He carries the umbrella and sees further despite his blind poetic eye that imagines me as a straight isotrope, or so it seemed once when the truth had a lightness of touch, before he grew so tall.

The boats go out, one, two, nineteen, thirty-four, each making straight for its allotted position in the strategy of sardines. So I com-pose my first and only poem in Portuguese for Manuel, five foot high and a poet:

As seis saiem os barcos:
Um barco, dois barcos, três barcos,
Quatro barcos, cinco barcos, seis barcos.

It can go on for ever to a transfinite number and Manuel recites it back at me with great appreciation when he serves the soup, to re-es-tablish the barcos relationship and no more between us. With other courses he gets too hot and busy but at coffee he sometimes recites his own poetry, though I can't tell whether he recites Camoens or himself. The rhythm sounds like himself.

The sea sounds like myself. The waves, wild in the previous moon but calm under this one, break from the night into separate white lines of foam that move rapidly forward to become one long white line before it vanishes on the dark sand. Over and over the separate lines merge into one and die. The high rocks floodlit in orange contrast the moon on the water and the small lights of the sardine fleet out there in the blackness. The beach at night deserted of its gay pullulating significance has no meaning but a strip of emptiness on which to land from which to sail although the army stands ghostly in the orange light, made up of slatted deckchairs in three regimented rows, folded against each untented pole. The army stands between two worlds, defending night from day, full emptiness from plenitude or loving from not loving.

Out of the miradouro on the promontory above the crackling loudspeaker flings its waves of music over the murmur of voices and the murmur of the sea and the white lines joining hands. The whole town sits up there and talks incessantly, a couple or two shuffles around in the night heat that prevents the frenzied dances of the North to the jukebox records from America, France and sometimes Spain that now wail out this summer's haunting hit 'La Pinta, la Niña, la Santa Maria'.

I sing a little with it on my dark ledge of stone which has kept the day-heat. Travellers need three ships between two worlds.

—You enjoying it?

All travellers need three ships between two worlds but I wish this one wouldn't pick on me. I don't nibble that easy though I fawn on those who hurt me and why don't you concentrate on me for a change says Crank and he carries the umbrella.

—Lovely isn't it?

—Laolita nao venga, I reply as nasally as I can under a suddenly adopted nationality and walk away towards and from la Pinta la Niña la Santa Maria in my head and the Quinta de Santo Antonio where the hotel stands, counting um barco, dois barcos, três barcos, trinta barcos working with their lights in the strategy of sardines.

So I sit and wait between courses in dark glasses, looking mysterious I hope and picking still at my *Epitaph of a Small Winner* in Portuguese to show off, or else to avoid la route de Saragosse. But the large elegant lady at the table next to mine flashes her splendid teeth all over her dark tan and I give up my fake nationality in a sentence or two. She flirts with Manuel out of her bulging eyes whenever she orders ice and I see myself at fifty-five if a day, under her fluffed-up dyed black hair, above her silk and pearls that flatter in triplicate her wrinkled neck. Perhaps he goes up to her room at night, she has seen life and runs a house in Lisbon.

—So you still invent stories about people? And I suppose you still insist on calling me Basil-the-boss?

—No. I can call you Felix if you like. I have a cousin called Felix who used to bully me and grew into a small sad man.

—Thank you.

—Well but you see you will change the image. He always has some calamity to relate. I said to him once, one day Felix, you will tell me a happy story. I haven't seen him since.

—Um barco, dois barcos, três barcos, says Manuel unexpectedly with the and chuckles.

—O que ě isto, Manuel? I can't eat those.

—Lulas.

—Lulas?

—Ja tem comido. Boa, boa.

—Bem, bem.

The language laughs at me. Felix's mother has departed. He taps only the left side of his nose now with his left forefinger as he waits for lulas. His young and swarthy wife talks in an animated way to Phoebe, and perhaps to Phoebe's thin dark husband who has his back to the dining room full of routes de Saragosse as the large elegant Lisbon lady who has seen life says Eu abro um casino aqui no primeiro de julho. Entiende? Um casino.

—Si! I struggle valiantly. Como se chama?

—Chama se . . . Casino.

She laughs a masculine laugh and flicks open her handbag, flashing her splendid teeth above the greenish pearls in triplicate, and out comes a yellow poster folded in four with the print visible on the wrong side. Empresa de Ferreira e Tomar it unfolds and she looks like an empress as the language laughs at me and the ground rushes away under my naked feet. Each wave crashes coolly around my ankles and recedes so fast it takes away my sense of balance, bringing it back just as my heels sink into the soft sand that rushes off again under my naked feet. Um barco, dois barcos, trinta barcos one by one return from the night strategy of sardines, and for some reason which I must invent a rowing boat weighed down by forty apostles or so makes for the shore. Henry the Navigator the Infanta sails for his tragic journey which he watches seated on his monument in the town, wearing a plumed biretta.

Every day at ten a.m. Flugzeug walks along the rock path down the steps to the beach in a striped towel dressing gown and a colonial helmet, carrying three inflated mattresses strapped round himself and followed by his women in order of age and plainness, in colonial helmets too. And every day at thirteen hundred hours and again at eighteen hundred he returns, Herr General with the baby-face, trudging the sand and wearily up the steps, strapped with inflated mattresses and followed by his women in order of age and plainness, remembering perhaps the retreat from Stalingrad. The route de Saragosse continues right across the French tables but now Fenella of the flaxen hair sits next to me and says something or other to her pink young husband Nigel surely, just like the chevalier sans peur et sans reproche.

—Sans what?

—You know, what they say about the knight.

—Which night?

—The chevalier sans peur et sans reproche.

—Sans what?

—Oh never mind.

—I can't hear darling, in all this noise. Did you quote Shakespeare or something?

—No, snails, she utters through her flaxen hair to the large elegant Lisbon lady who has seen life and keeps trying to get into their conversation as they now sit between us. You know, with a little house.

—Uma casa?

—Yes, and horns.

—Não . . . ?

—Horns, you know, like this. Goes very slowly. What's slowly darling?

Mooty tempo.
—Ah.
—The French eat them. Franceses . . . eat.
—Ah si! Casa. Restaurante . . . Eu abro um casino aqui no primeiro de julho. Entende? Um casino.
—Owe, a casinowe? How interesting.
Nigel and Fenella have youth and flaxen hair and easy prospects. He fishes underwater with a receding chin but she has more money and intelligence in her eyes and more flaxen hair. He does well, however, in the city. He does well, rather, in the property business. They have two lovely children, one boy, one girl.
—Do you always invent stories about people you'll never see again? says Basil-the-boss in the restaurant, hotel, casino who cares.
—Sometimes the stories come true. Not always. Sometimes I get to know the people and they turn out much duller.
—Did you invent a story about me?
—Oh yes. Before we met.
—Before we met? Oh, you mean at first sight?
—No I mean sight unseen.
—I hope I came up to expectations. Tell it to me.
—No. A banal story doesn't bear the telling.
—I see. I hope I didn't come up to expectations then.
—Or the living. But you had no name. Only a sort of label.
—Oh. Dangerous things, labels. They come between people.
—Yes, two, says Fenella lifting two fingers. Dois.
—Dois meninos? Formosos, sim?
—They're very wicked.
—Como?
—They're . . . what's wicked darling? Er . . . you know, wicked. Er diablos.
—Ah si! Bem . . . bem.
She flashes her splendid teeth that flatter her sun tanned neck in triplicate under her bulging eyes and fluffed-up dyed black hair. Little does she know that as a medium-man I have tumbled her in the shape

of a Brazilian Irrigation Engineer.

—Quatro barcos, cinco barcos, seis barcos says Manuel to re-establish the poetic relationship and no more between us.

And then I notice Julho de Janeiro. He truly deserves the name in a pink shirt open to the waist demanding love for the golden glow of god-like beauty which I know at once will not melt me but men. Nevertheless I wax and in my mind he executes five entrechats above the murmuring waves. Above the crashing waves even. He sits on the veranda with a tense thin little man like Nijinski in the second phase of madness. Then the god rises suddenly revealing pale blue shorts and muscular golden legs, walks in the third position through the dining room as if about to float a ballerina up above his self-love and the marvelling audience. He wears a heavy ivory charm on his chest bared by the pink shirt. He sits two tables to my left, facing the room like me, like the Lady Fenella on my right and the Brazilian Irrigation Engineer who has seen life on my left. So I lose sight of him and see only Nijinski in the second phase of madness.

—All the ladies to the wall says Nigel in a loud upper accent to Fenella of the flaxen hair.

You grow into a hotel room after a while. You possess it with your aspects, you spread your little habits over it and they take root. The underwear goes in the second drawer, the beachwear and the unused cardigan in the third, the anti-mosquito cream, calamine lotion suntan oil silver pink nail varnish wait on your needs inside the cupboard, the bottle of mineral water on the crochet mat of the bedside table, poderosamente radio-activas, liticas, arsenicais, fluoretadas gasocarbonicas, together with your *Epitaph of a Small Winner* by Machado de Assis and the miniature red dictionary. The blue washbasin in the shower cubicle stands on one leg, your wet green swimsuit hangs on the balcony rail with the wet blue towel, the agaves spike out of the golden rock into the sky and so on out of time. You only buy a little local colour your mind with it and live in a suspension of belief and disbelief.

You move. To another room along the corridor perhaps, to another hotel, village, town, and even from along the corridor that room has lost your aspects and your underwear, your calamine lotion and your *Epitaph*. You carry your case away, your sun-hat and your powerfully radioactive water.

You move into a new relationship or two. Lolita, Phoebe, Fátima, Herr General, the Brazilian Irrigation Engineer or Lisbon lady who has seen life opens a casino and Fenella and sad Felix vanish like things out of your head and new things come.

They walk along the beach in French. From the back the tall one looks like a well-made man except for the bikini strap not all that necessary from the front. She walks a masculine stride with feminine grace and dramatised gestures around their discourses over shells and rocks, regardez ça, je dois vous dire, jamais de ma vie, mais croyez-moi, bien sûr under the curly grisonnant crop. She listens too with the poised attention of a handsome lover sure of himself and kind. The short one looks less brown, more female, she bulges and her clipped silver rinse flies untidily in the breeze. They both wear wedding rings.

Joaquím smiles with enormous understanding. The sand rushes away as we walk behind them, overtake their discourses, walk along and behind them. He strides in the third position and each wave caresses our ankles then recedes so fast it takes away my sense of balance and brings it back as I sink my heels into the soft wet sand that rushes away again.

—I think she teaches eurythmics, I say to Joaquím in French. Vous connaissez? La rythmique.

—Non, non. Moi, le ballet classique. Deuxième danseur dans . . .

—Please do me an entrechat, Joaquím.

To my chagrin despite my *Epitaph* I can't understand a word he says in Portuguese. But his self-love absorbs all the homage I can't give to men and which therefore men don't give me, he drinks it up like a hungry child, he accepts it simply like an avid young god and I give on out of boundless resources suddenly unstemmed. I want and expect nothing and he knows it. So we play ball in the wet sand and when he jumps to catch it with an entrechat the big ivory charm on his chest jumps on its chain.

—What is it, Joaquím, let me see.

The carving shows a bearded man with three fingers up, and out of him a swaddled baby sitting on a bird.

—Ou Santo Spirito.

—Muite formoso. Como Joaquím.

He inclines his head courteously, looks at me with flitting wonder then laughs and leaps into the sea.

Nijinski whose name is Jules smatters excellently in German English French Dutch Spanish and Portuguese, in which he addresses all their dining neighbours to tease Joaquím as if to say you may have beauty and talent but I have travelled wide and all the world loves me, and me to say you may have the power of the medium-man over me but I have another self my female brother in me and I love him. Jules and I get on fine. Their dining neighbours include chiefly me for everyone has vanished like things out of my head and new things come.

They walk on the dusty road in the hot sun, dressed all in black with black scarves on their head. The tallest of the three carries the black umbrella.

—She'll make herself ill, says the fattest of the three, bouncing about in the hot sun, reading her *Epitaph* and rendering homage.

—She cheats, though, says the thinnest and most angular, with a descent from space into new matter.

—Not entirely new, says the tallest and most knowing, she takes old aspects with her sun-hat and her poderosamente radioactive waters, liticas, arsenicais, fluoretadas, gasocarbonicas.

—The sun burns everywhere, says the fattest and most panting. She won't escape.

—Not everywhere, says the tallest. I carry the umbrella and can see further, despite my blind eye.

—Look, Joaquím. Les Trois Destinées.

—Oui? Fados. Très noires. Pretas.

—Oh but they bring luck. Like your charm. They will make you very famous, and promote you from second dancer to first dancer.

—Moi, vingt ans seulement. Deuxième danseur.

—And you will travel all over the world and the world will acclaim you and love you.

—Oh, oui.

He beams in my attention, which at once erases the crumpled look he wears during Jules's exclusion through smattering to the world.

Some French do not talk of la route de Saragosse. Some Germans do not retreat from Stalingrad. Some Italians don't sing. Some English do not condescend their friendship or complace you all over with their complacency. Innumerable wives do not nibble at medium-men and love the man they love but they don't include me. Some men see more than sunflowers or daisies on the way, more than straight isotropes that don't exist or ideal numbers that: undoubtedly divide the prime which by definition have no dividers but themselves and unity. At first I tried to imagine myself a medium-man who nibbles at me and suddenly spews me forth like ectoplasm, but some undoubtedly don't even nibble except possibly other people who don't feel or talk like that at all and have different names if indeed they exist. But now I drown in the particular. I only buy a little local colour, crisp as a biscuit, wafer-thin, it will vanish like things out of my head and new things come. I love my brother Joaquím, my own self-love who lifts me above the world of men like a sylphide and will deposit me gently on the tip of one toe and twirl me round into the fifth perspective.

I don't understand lovers' quarrels in Portuguese. Jules and Joaquím pick at each other in haranguing undertones. Joaquím tosses his head and petulates his mouth and makes big blue eyes at everyone until he suddenly wears a crumpled look as Jules withdraws his haranguing adoration and smatters to the world he has travelled and which loves him more than Joaquím.

—I think I'll go to Tangiers, he says to me in English to exclude Joaquím.

—Tangiers? I say in French to include Joaquím and it rhymes with danger.

—Do you know how long it takes to get from Ayamonte to Algeciras he goes on in English.

—Well . . . But I know neither the kilometres nor enough French or Portuguese so end up unconvincingly um dia.

—So long! Impossible.

—Well, half a day perhaps I concede looking at Joaquím in pink and orange tonight, who doesn't touch his soup and wears a crumpled look. Two hours perhaps to Cadiz I say in French and three hours to Algeciras, by bus, I mean, as far as I remember. He says I'll go tomorrow.

—You'll go? What about Joaquím?

The crumpled look remains despite the return of attention and the blue eyes go limpid in the bronzed god face surely too young for more than momentary anguish.

—Joaquím has to do his military service. Yes. I think go to Tangiers.

—When?

—Tomorrow perhaps. Or the day after.

—I mean, when does Joaquím, Joaquím when do you have to do your military service?

—Quintaferia. Dans trois jours.

—But, how ridiculous! What about your dancing? Why, they'll send you to Angola.

—Moi, soldat magnifique.

—Yes but three days, good heavens, Joaquím! Jules, why don't you stay here with him? His last three days.

Jules shrugs and Joaquím whips out his dark glasses despite the electric light where I wear mine no longer. Jules talks to me about Tangiers and Tetuán, the Arab quarters, André Gide and *The Seven Pillars of Wisdom*. A big tear falls from under Joaquím's dark glasses into the untouched soup, and then another, and a third. Joaquím gets up quickly, silently, and walks out of the room in pink and orange and the third position slightly muted.

—Jules, why do you torment Joaquím? Because he has more beauty and talent than you?

—Huh! He behaves like a spoilt child.

—But Jules, you love him as a spoilt child, as a beautiful doll, you can't have it both ways.

—He can't bear not to attract all the attention all of the time.

—We none of us can. But why should he have to learn to bear it like the rest of us mortals?

—You worship him, don't you?

I worship Joaquím. On quintaferia jeudi Thursday Joaquím lies naked on my bed and I make love to him. He takes and I give nothing of myself, my lips not on his lips. He wants no naked femininity from me except my massive sandy hair unloosed all over him, my blanches-mains now browned, their fingertips under the silver pink working quickly gently as I watch a young god lying like a woman and rising like a man. And when I have paid my homage and my tribute, more satisfying than the quick time of the busy medium-man who snatches sex and asks the routine question and doesn't stay for an answer, Joaquím puts my head on his loins and wipes himself on my unloosed hair. With this concession to my femininity he gets up, washes, dresses carefully, preens himself a little, kisses my brow and vanishes into the night, the army and his young god's second or first dancer's fame beyond.

The moon balances on the promontory of orange rock, orange and big. The sea sounds like myself. I walk on the dark beach in French and bits of Portuguese as the moon leaps up the sky and lights the sea. I let the waves lap at my ankles and can't see the sand rushing away as I sink my heels to keep my sense of balance, then lose it with my face up at the stars that hang low and innumerable as transfinite numbers over the boats answering them in the silent strategy of sardines. I have moved out of the particular, out of the routes de Saragosse, Herr General, Felix of the tapped nose and João, Fátima, Lolita and the large elegant O Casino lady who has seen life and Irrigation perhaps and Nigel, Fenella of the flaxen hair, Jules, Joaquím, Basil-the-boss, Quinta-la-blonde-aux-blanches-mains that conjure up black sails on far horizons, out of the nonexistent isotropes and ideal numbers that divide the indivisible, out of trying to imagine myself a medium-man who has no name or number and merely acquires my vices with which I destroy Crank who says you display your enthusiasms like frilly underwear to those who treat you with every discourtesy and pay you back with the same sullen indifference you give to me.

I lie alone, my sandy hair unloosed on the dark sand and hear the sea crashing inside the caverns under the high rock. The moon sails up towards the stars at the lightning speed of years between nothing and nothing. I lie on the wet sand, between two days, two worlds, lifted by my self-love into the perspective, gently deposited on a southern tip near where the statue of Henry the Navigator the Infanta in his stone plumed biretta sails all night, watching himself and listening to the murmuring calculations of total emptiness.

Queenie Fat and Thin

Queenie was short, and on the fat side of plump when she lived on bread and butter and potatoes and baked beans in a coffin of a room behind Earls Court. That was ten years ago. She must have been around forty then, but she dressed little girl, in fluffed-out hair and gathered skirts that thickened her thick waist, drawing the eye rather to the low necklines with their hint of carnal promise as she talked about the reality of angels in her daily life, the nous-sphere or what happens to the decision we do not take, the course we do not choose, does it continue to exist in the mind of God as it once existed in ours.

I love Queenie. Not in fact carnally despite the sometimes hint of promise with a surprisingly small breast or two apparent in the low neckline when she bends or even when she does not. I prefer hidden treasures. And I like fat to go with large, and thin with small, I like correct proportions. Besides I have a statuesque wife whom I love in that way, witness our nine children who might not exist as far as Queenie is concerned, indeed, three of them did not at the time. No, I love Queenie as one loves, well, not exactly a spirit, nor as one loves a child, but something in between, a sprite perhaps, a metaphysical sprite tumbling about in all that slightly excess flesh. I'd like to tumble you Queenie I'd say in my wife's presence, which actually I did not, or a cruder word, just to see the mock-maidenly distress in her nut-coloured wide-set eyes interlace with coyness, the quick pale flutter of lashes, the pursed Clara Bow lips before she lit another cigarette.

That was ten years ago before Queenie became famous and thin. She would spend hours with us, down in the country where I have my practice, and often days and nights, even weeks once, after her nervous breakdown from the strain of trying to live on her contributions to

Spiral--The Organ of Fantastic Realism, everything is a spiral she said, the galaxies, the thread of life, the history of knowledge and the neurological system. And although I was not her doctor I looked after her in every way I could, listening to her and making her eat lean steaks voraciously to make up for the potatoes and baked beans. Not that my wife didn't give her those as well, with six children to look after I can't expect her to be an imaginative cook besides.

Queenie is critical of Gwen, despite or maybe because of our six children whose vulgar existence she ignores with a look of distaste at such Old Testament profusion saying it was all right in those days when the earth was barren but you don't have to go forth and multiply *now*. She pronounces *now* primly, as if to go on elocution-like how-now-brown-cow of Gwen, making her feel like a productive cow, but if you must have many then have nine, not six, nine is a holy number, gazing at Gwen as at an apparition and indeed she has that air of genuine first-everness whatever she gazes at. Ow, I doo like that dress, she says, you look like a Welsh witch in that homespun weave and long black straight hair. A nice Welsh witch of course, a cosy sort of Welsh witch, harmless, like the Druids. Did you know that the Druids, the original ones I mean, never met at Stonehenge at all, but in wood groves? It's true that Gwen, though statuesque, looks arty, which she isn't at all, but motherly and domestic, with a sweet patient smile that masks the hurt of Queenie's wonder-wrapped barbs. They pretend to be mesolithic, the modern ones I mean, they say they've kept alive the mysteries of the Old Religion. But of course it was a mother-earth religion, chthonic you know, whereas they come and watch the sunrise at midsummer among phallic stones. Well I ask you, Julian. And she flutters her pale lashes at me under bright red fluffed-up hair, then laughs what she calls her silvery laugh which means like tinkling coppers in a male pocket don't you think Julian, after all who ever heard of a silvery laugh, and she bends to smooth a wrinkle of her stocking on a thick short shin, showing the hint of carnal promise within the low-cut neckline. Surprisingly small however, considering the surplus fat elsewhere. I prefer hidden treasures, such as the airy dream behind her nut-coloured eyes, that glimpses out in sudden strange remarks as if a metaphysical sprite in touch with ghosts, angels and mesolithic mother-goddesses tumbled about somewhere in all that slightly excess flesh for such a short pale person. But what do you suppose happens to all that flesh, when a fat man slims down?

She stares inconsequentially at my thin wiriness, meaning I think when a statuesque woman slims, for instance Gwen, who perhaps needs to, and I prepare a swift medical reply that evaporates like lost weight as she adds: from the point of view, I mean, of the Resurrection.

—The Resurrection?

—The Resurrection of the flesh of course. I mean, at what age and in what shape will God choose to resurrect us? Fat and forty or slim and seventeen? I was quite sylphlike at seventeen. No Julian, not as children, they're too unformed and boring, evil in fact, it wouldn't be fair, the myth of childish innocence has long been exploded, besides, they haven't enough flesh. I think thirty-three, man's perfect age you know, Christ died at thirty-three, the Trinity you see, a third of ninety-nine, I wasn't bad looking at thirty-three. She flutters her pale lashes at me, makes her Clara Bow mouth, nervously stubbing out a cigarette between dumpy lingers, her nails all brittle and splitting at the edge. Queenie needs calcium.

Yes, I love Queenie. Her own doctor had given her iron and calcium tablets, and sedatives to stop her sudden inexplicable tears such as her angels weep when she feels low she says. She has five angels, one on each shoulder to guard her right and sinister instincts, oh yes the sinister has to be guarded too, the right can't exist without it, didn't you know? One in the head, in the pituitary gland to be precise, that's for imagination, or do I mean the thalamus, and he's the angel of instant communication. With what? Well, God of course. The pineal gland? Of course not. Yes I know Descartes placed the soul there but he was wrong wasn't he, what do you expect from a rationalist, besides, science has advanced since then. And one behind in the central nervous system, he's the Recording Angel, he records all my sins as committed by the fifth, the Dark Angel, who's in the womb, he envies sex, angels have none you see. All my sins are of the flesh.

Which do not include children or even love of them. She is being ana-lysed for thyroid deficiency and the radioactive iodine went right through my angels she says and they laughed, tickled to death by the tracing isotopes. Well, not to death, angels can't die. Her basic metabol-ism rate is below 27 but her thyroid is normal, so for that matter is the pituitary. The gynaecologist says she has fibroids and recommends an eventual hysterectomy should they increase though not essential now, a bit drastic to my mind, and where would the angel dwell she asks? In fact Queenie lacks nothing except fame and thinness, though her ovari-an system shows a slight imbalance which is soon rectified.

And these she acquires, not exactly overnight but fast and suddenly nevertheless. The fame comes first, and the thinness ensues, naturally enough, since thinness seldom in itself can entail fame. How right, she says, still fat and only slightly famous, that a past mistress in the nous-sphere should win fame overnight in the swansong of radio. But I shall never appear on television. I don't believe in television do you? The visual image ruins the imagination. By which I think she means she is too fat, pursing her lips all coyly Clara Bow and fluttering her pale eye-lashes as she laughs like tinkling copper in a male pocket, showing a hint or two of carnal promise.

I feel pleased at my diagnosis, prognosis and therapeutic recom-mendation in the swansong of radio and pre-menopausal breakdown. It is I who push her, bully her as only a doctor can after one of her weep-ing spells, to put her name down as a local questioner for the visiting team of Twenty Questions me? She sobs, but I have no questions, it's the answers that bother me Julian can't you understand? Oh come on Queenie, you ask questions all day, but even as I say it I realise that she never asks questions but produces answers in question form ending didn't you know? And if her certainties beg even larger questions she seems only a quarter aware of it in that wide-eyed lash-fluttering nut-coloured look of wonder and first-ever apparition of a bright idea, a ghost, a mother-goddess, angel or minister of grace, unless merely an object in the house, not a child of course, but a pincushion say, made by

Gwen, how quaint, ow how lovely Gwen, aren't you clever, I couldn't do
thet, or my own personal phallically thick Parker pen without which I
can't write prescriptions in correct illegibility, ow, I leyke *thet*, Julian,
can I hev it? I'll give you meyn, and gone is my correct medical illegibility for evermore.

She dries her eyes, clumsily surrounds them with a hard black frame
and preens herself for hours. I look so fet, she wails, how can I ask a
question? Queenie dear you look marvellous my wife says and anyway
no one will see you on radio, ow, how-now-brown-cow says Queenie's
look and I interject quickly Queenie I could tumble you right now.
Really? She Clara-Bows me flutters and so forth you have a devil in you
Julian, Gwen, your husband has a devil in him did you know, and goes.

She asks, of course, a parasensory question, I forget which, curiously
enough, considering what it leads to, fame, thinness and all that ensues
from those; not starting like the others, in view of the fact three com-
plicated clauses does the team think, but something utterly unearthly
or is it Rosicrucian or the New Unknown that held already all the
present knowledge of modern science in India over two thousand years
ago but kept it secret for the good of humanity because only the spiritu-
ally upright unlike modern physicists ought to possess the Truth in her
prim piping voice. No, it can't have been that, but I remember the prim
piping voice, the embarrassed silence and the meandering of the panel
members for once paralysed in their smart attempts to evade questions
and sum up the world with momentary wit. And then, unprecedentally
she answers back, her precise piping certainties disguised as wouldn't
you say didn't you know isn't that what you meant? In the swansong of
radio such odd behaviour gets into all the papers as a one-minute wonder and her round face with fluffed-up bright red hair that comes out
black disturbs her image of herself to tears that interlace the pleasure
and mock-surprise in the Clara Bow pursed mouth. And in no time at all
she joins the panel, travelling around, answering questions like in view
of the fact that the Government, the Council, the doctors, the Employ-
ment Tax, the brain-drain, the trade-gap, the pop groups, the wilful de-
struction of telephone booths, the danger on the roads does the team

think, with radiating angels of energy through matter travelling faster than light and healing powers that even Christ and others used after all by transmitting electricity through hands into the nervous system made up as we all know of electrical neural cells that affect willpower and could change the world as humanity mutates into the nous-sphere and reaches spiritual fullness although we may have to pass through government by secret societies of adepts first, cryptocracy you know, it has already happened in a way, not among politicians who are illiterate in the new language of energy but among physicists, they are the alchemists, who have always known the secret truth, but unlike the alchemists they do not practise spiritual regeneration, I mean they do not let the transmutation of elements also transmute the experimenter as the observer affects the object observed why, that's a scientific fact, but they have lost the original secret bond between mind and matter so that it's only a one-way traffic now which is immensely dangerous. Queenie becomes a personality.

We do not see much of Queenie for a time. Not that she is uppish or anything, at least not in absentiae, but doctors, even as friends, get used to losing sight and sound of patients who no longer need them. It is a mark of success, in a way, Queenie's success, however, being no longer mine, even if I feel, now and then, a small proprietary right in it.

When we do have sight and sound of her again, it comes in the small box as quite a shock. Gwen can't get over it. She stares into the set allowing Cathy's private parts to gape out from the unpinned nappy as the flickering image suddenly possesses the living room. But that's not Queenie she says, it can't be, though the name appears almost subliminally below the narrow face, the sleek dark hair and the sophisticated plunging neckline, only to vanish as Gwen repeats it can't be, she's so thin. But the piping voice is uttering its airy propositions and we know, Queenie has made it.

We are glad. I am glad. I rejoice for Queenie in her fame and thinness, she lacking nothing else, not even iodine, iron, calcium, children, earthiness, although her sins, she says, are of the flesh. And what has happened to all that flesh, from the point of view, I mean, of the Resurrection?

So we drive up to London, Gwen and I, on the spur of a sudden desire to see her in her fame and thinness, to congratulate her, to find out. She has moved her personality from the coffin of a room in Earls Court to a new flat and Mrs. Gloster, Mrs. Glossary as Queenie used to call her on account of the words she uses says no, she has strictly vowed on all that she holds eminent in her heart and soul not to divulge. But after a many-such-worded while she relents for the sake of the old days when after all Queenie had amity for you doctor she says, even a temporal obsession you might call it doctor like a malady for she discoursed upon you frequently and your dear wife of course and gentlemanly profusion when you gave her counsel and calcium as a turning pivot in her career. Oh yes she has done well, our Queenie has.

She has done so well that she is out, a plain girl tells us at the door, and we retire into the car to write a note which takes longer than expected owing to my new thick Parker pen and renewed medical illegibility Gwen says and a new care with words in a crestfallen spirit that gazes into the driving-mirror to see, petite and slim and copper-haired, in an elegant purple suit trimmed with mink, a little lady emerge from a sidedoor, look carefully up and down the street and then trip forth high-heeled as I leap out, march up and stop in glad amazement Queenie! And fury blazes from the wide-set nut-coloured eyes skillfully rimmed in copper eyelashes.

—Julian you mustn't, ow you really mustn't. Who do you think you are barging up from the provinces without an appointment?

—But Queenie—

—Ay'm a very busy woman, Julian, even the silliest interviewing journalist knows that. You think you can presume on the old days, but the old days have gone, I've changed since then.

—I can see that . . . Queenie you look marvellous. So slim. How did you do it?

The old pleased coyness for a moment interlaces the anger in those wide-set nut-coloured eyes skilfully framed in copper lashes and the pink lipstick creases as the mouth Clara-Bows, briefly though, I suffer she says. It's very slimming. And the old Queenie glances out, subliminally and gone, I'd be willing to see you at another more convenient time if you make an appointment with my secretary. Goodbye.

Letters, in my phallically thick medical illegibility, ensue, with briefly typewritten replies. Time passes, to be followed, Gwen prophesies like a Welsh witch, by an emotional outburst in a personal spidery scrawl, and so it happens, despite my melancholy disbelief, five pages of it to match her angels perhaps or some Pythagorean number in the mysterious electricity of her neural cells that work like all things spiralwise, paranoiac, shrill and sad, spiralling through into one ear and out the other hardly touching my heart or do I mean memory for my heart is wrung but I will not remember since time heals as well, better than iron and calcium, iodine, earthiness, electric hands, fame and thinness. Where has it gone, I write briefly, all that flesh, in which the airy sprite that was you seemed to tumble, but now has vanished with it, from the point of view, I mean, of the Resurrection? But Queenie gives no answer, even disguised as question, and I expect none.

Her parasensory certainties still seduce the nation with glimpses of the new unknown that flicker blue-grey from the box and become household words. But have they acquired a certain patina, I ask Gwen who agrees with all I say thus increasing my doubts, are they perhaps a shade mechanical, professional, gimmicky, lacking the old spontaneity or am I imagining the evaporation of the airy sprite in all that flesh? Her sins, Gwen says with the placid wisdom of how now brown cow, were of the flesh, not of the spirit presumably she meant but when the flesh goes what sins are there left? Do you mean, I ask in disbelief, that she now leads a virtuous life despite the larger hints of smaller carnal promise in the more daring necklines almost below the framework of the box in the sophisticated circles she moves in? That's as may be Gwen says flatly, she certainly looks more desirable but all I know is that the flesh is gone. So I feel mortally afraid.

But I too am a busy man not mortally afraid for long what with nine and a half children and their woes including measles, mumps, lack of attention and exams according to age and temperament, patients and their woes from puberty to geriatry. It is then that I receive the picture from a rich lady whom I have helped through the menopause with more involvement than medical etiquette would approve, but then, one has to judge these things and the discretion of the other party and I judged that slight involvement was the better part of therapy in the particular case. Mind you, not a Picasso, she says, or anything valuable, as if to imply that getting through the menopause with pleasure is not worth a Picasso since she might have got through it with pleasure anyway, but a young unknown I have taken under my protection who might prove quite an investment for you after all, Julian, in your old age, I'm buying all his pictures. And I like the picture, Picasso notwithstanding, it reminds me of Queenie with blue spirals in stucco plaster on a sea-green background full of copper circles that change colour as I walk past it up and down in the small living room it soon outgrows.

Last week we saw Queenie again. She had just published *Spirals*, a ghosted collection of her metaphysical telly-aphorisms selling like hot electricity on account of her fame and thinness, and after a large publication party well reported in the press she gave a smaller one for some of her old friends, as a gesture perhaps for none of her new friends was there except her agent and her secretary as if to say you wouldn't mix but to-forget-old-friends, unless be-nice-to-everyone-on-the-way-up, you-may-need-them-on-the-way-down. But no, I am lacking in charity, only stage people say that, Queenie wouldn't. Or can't envisage a way down.

So there we are, an odd assortment including the two editors of *Spiral —Organ of Fantastic Realism*, and me and Gwen unusually elegant in a new expensive dress chosen with great care, ow, what a sweet frock says Queenie. She herself just back from Stockholm or San Francisco or somewhere in a Chardin model no not Chardin d'you like this little Dior thing she asks, and prances small and slim in black mousseline with a loose panel in front, under which her well manicured hands needing no calcium now would vanish to fondle her trim tum, I call it my nun's habit she says and this, out come the well-manicured hands again to finger the deep cleavage inside a diamond shaped window cut over the more than glimpse of carnal promise, this is the Valley of Temptation.

I smile with momentary relief. Queenie is there again, the metaphysical imp tumbling in the considerably less flesh of the new groomed slim self-assured but no less enchanting personality she has become. Momentary only, though, for as I hear her repeat the same remark to every group of guests she moves among like a perfect hostess, I become aware of a great lack, as of the sprite in all that slightly excess flesh. You never answered my question, Queenie. I never answer any questions as you know Julian, what was it? Well, where has it gone? You know, from the point of view of the Resurrection? Oh that. You mustn't presume on the old days, Julian, as if to say with almost tears of anger or fear in her skilfully copper-framed eyes you mustn't upset me now. Well, tell me at least, as a doctor, I'm interested to know, how did you lose it all, so quickly I mean? I told you, I suffered. I stopped eating, that's all. And with this concession to the old days between us she goes on to talk of how cheap was the hotel suite she had in Paris, and Dior models and how much she paid for the diamond ring she shows me and the first-class airfares across the Atlantic so much more room, she says, only a hundred pounds more, why, I can earn that in a week.

Yes, the old Queenie has gone, or rather, as I had at first imprecisely surmised in front of the flickering blue-grey image in my living room, the old Queenie gets hoarded up, channelled for profit, fame and thinness under the bright lights, before the cameras that carry the numerously multiplied blue-grey image into each and every other living room, while Queenie in the flesh is vain, self-centred, vulgar, no, she was all those things before, but now she is all those things and dull. I know where the metaphysical sprite tumbling in all that slightly excess flesh has gone. The monster has swallowed it up.

Or has it? Queenie came down to see us yesterday, unannounced in a Jaguar Mark IV driven by a young Tibetan chauffeur and carrying her agent, her plain secretary, her beautician and a new sable coat. They sip tea in the small living room and do not touch the crumpets served by Gwen distressed in a Welsh-witch dress of homespun weave, only for housework and the minding of the children by way of explanation. But

Queenie's eyes are on my menopausal picture. Ow, she says, I leyke thet Julian. It has no value of course but yes, I leyke it, can I hev it? It's yours I say Spanish style and even half mean it.

Today the Tibetan chauffeur has come in the Jaguar Mark IV and taken the menopause away with its spirals in blue stucco plaster on the deep green background full of copper circles that change colour as I walk past it up and down in the small living room. Where has it gone, I wonder, from the point of view, I mean, of the Resurrection?

Go When You See the Green Man Walking

says a woman's voice.

The woman has guessed her language, here in the strange city at the traffic lights. Has guessed her nationality from what, her blonde hair no there are blonde women in this country also and hairdressers. From her clothes then driving clothes crumpled cotton shirt and skirt and canvas shoes that had stepped forward too fast, drawn by a lull in traffic, before the green man had appeared.

She draws back saying thank you in her language and the woman smiles. She is elegantly dressed in a white linen suit and an expensive silk blouse, white leather shoes composed of heel and toecap only, leaving the slim foot bare.

The red man stands, rectangular legs apart, luminous. In her country they have discs only, green amber red. Excuse-me in her language if I am indiscreet but I want to buy some clothes. Good clothes. Could you direct me perhaps?

The woman smiles again or the same smile perhaps worn like makeup. Balassine. Cross over turn right and into that arcade you can just see it. Shoes Valentino's you go through the arcade turn left the other side. Shoes are very important with a glance down at the plimsoll types. The green man walks. His legs are also rectangular as if in trousers with square shoes now we can go.

Thank you very much.

Would you like me to come with you?

She stops on the other side staring at the stranger who could be herself. It is difficult in a strange country. Or perhaps difficult always yes? You make mistakes? They hang in cupboard not put on for years? Directing their steps towards the arcade. But she can't spend that much on a blouse, a suit perhaps yes but a mere blouse what will she wear it with it means buying a suit to match or at least a really good skirt or silk trousers at some even more fantastic price it doesn't even look expensive.

And a dark blue silk suit at an even more fantastic price.

And shoes to match. Valentino shoes.

Handbag, leather gloves.

Crazy earrings.

It's a good buy says the elegant foreign lady you will not regret. You're very welcome. Goodbye.

In the strange city very unwelcome sitting alone on a dark hotel balcony, smoking a cigarette, watching the empty street and the traffic lights change from the green man walking to the red man standing and back. The warm air floats between her skin and nightdress like soft caressing hands. A dark red car cuts the corner and corrects its direction just in time to avoid a white one which stops with a screech of brakes at the red man standing. The screech of brakes has been perhaps muffled by the distance between the car and the third-floor balcony of the hotel. The white car waits interminably, purring or is it growling in the warm night air, as the green man walks for no traffic on the transverse street. The green man flashes on for him and he turns right slowly then pulls up. A girl demure in a white longsleeved high-necked blouse and a navy blue skirt steps out from under the arches and walks up to the car, bends forward to speak to the driver through the window, hand on hip left leg crooked out although he surely cannot see the legs from the driver's seat on the other side. A moment passes of presumably conversation. She shrugs and walks back to her corner, the car drives off. She stands outside the illuminated shop underwear is it beneath the arches. Something tall turns slowly round behind her, a tower of brassieres perhaps on a swivelling turntable. The girl turns round to look into the window but not for long. She stands a demure schoolgirl in navy blue and white, the blouse of white lace tight-fitting flattering her breasts, her skirt short the weight of her body on her left leg, the right leg crooked out forwards to show the inside of her thigh, her right hand on her hip, her left hand holding a navy blue handbag with a white cardigan folded into the strap. Her hair is long and black, curling over her shoulders.

Three boys pass by. One stops. He has broad shoulders in a brown leather jacket and narrow legs in jeans. The others hover round the corner, waiting. The boy who stopped talks to the girl then walks on and rejoins the others.

The red man stands with legs apart for no traffic.

The green man walks.

An orange-yellow car glides by, hesitates, turns the corner and stops.

The girl walks up to it. Same position, same presumably conversation, same result. She walks back to her corner outside the illuminated shop as the car drives off. It is a bookshop, a haze of pale rectangles in irregular positions. The girl scholastic-looking in navy blue and white turns to look into the window but not for long. She stands, patiently watching, patiently watched from the dark balcony. Behind her in the window a round tower of books swivels slowly round on a turntable. The red man stands, the green man walks.

From her left under the arcade the boy in the leather jacket comes back, alone. They talk, presumably. She shrugs and stretches her right arm in an indifferent gesture. He walks on.

A balding man waits on the pavement below the hotel. His bald top shines in the street lighting. The red man stands with legs apart, the balding man waits foreshortened from this angle and the girl shifts her slight weight to her other leg, crooking out her left. The balding man crosses despite the red man standing and walks up to the girl. They talk presumably. He looks her over, hesitates, talks again then walks on.

The warm air floats between her skin and nightdress like soft caressing hands.

She lights another cigarette, a very thin one now, thermometer thin and short, two inches, tapering at each end with a minute twist of the diagonally rolled paper. The girl below does not look up at the brief flame, a mere flicker in the neon and out. She inhales deeply, holds it, then out into the soft warm air that floats between her nightdress and her skin.

The nose of a white car has halted silently at the hotel corner. An open green sports car roars past the bookshop, turns right and stops, muttering like distant machine gun fire. The driver has thick blond hair or is it grey in the street lighting and wears an open-necked yellow shirt. He yanks his head hither at the girl and she walks to the car, bends forward one hand on the low door the other on her hip and legs apart. He shakes his head. She starts walking away and he drives off. The green man walks again for the transverse street and the white car edges forward, stops, the girl turns round, walks back and bends towards the window, same position, same presumably conversation, same result.

The girl stands outside the bookshop, framed in litup books, young as the night, and warm.

The air caresses her skin beneath the nightdress.

The books stand out now sharply in the shop window, bright in garish colours, cyclamen purple yellow red blue green that had seemed a pale haze before. She can see the lettering of the titles in a foreign language.

The green man walks again for the traffic from the right. But there is no traffic. A car has stopped with a jerk and pig-squeal on the transverse street to the left of the hotel corner. The red man stands the green man walks the car which is dark blue glides off and past the girl into the unseen street beyond the bookshop.

A small and tousled man in a creased check shirt and dirty cotton trousers bounces silently across the street. All the men look foreshortened until they get to the other side. He stops by the girl under the arcade, he has his back to the hotel at first then turns half way as he speaks to her, his glasses shining in the bookshop light. The girl suddenly steps out briskly with him back in the direction he has come from despite the luminous red man standing. They vanish round the corner her sharp steps clocking loud to his swift rubber soles.

The street is deserted. The green man flashes for no car. The red man stands his legs apart. A big black limousine glides across from the left and disappears beyond the bookshop corner.

Go when you see the green man walking.

She rises puts out the minute stub of her thin cigarette now fully smoked, rises from her chair, enters the dark room. In the blue gleam of light from the street she finds the switch by the big double bed, a gold light flashes on with a big bang that fumbles on as ground bass to high violins. She takes on her nightdress without drawing the curtains. She stands before the wardrobe mirror which reflects the blue light from the street behind her and the low yellow light from the bed. The two glows outline her silhouette in silvery gold, the pale hair dark against the light but framed in a haze of luminous yellow. The haze falls on the long hair that flicks up and the hair feathers her shoulders. In profile her breasts seem halved the nipples on fire. She strokes her hands firmly down her taut body, over the breasts and below. The skin is soft as silk. Once only. She opens the wardrobe and with a screech of agony her image vanishes. Inside hangs the new expensive blouse, its colours which had been soft and subtle catching the mingled light in bright turquoise gold, purple orange against the musty darkness inside. And the new dark silk suit almost invisible against the blouse in the dim light.

She takes the blouse from its hanger and puts it on soft and silky as the warm air on her bare skin. She buttons it halfway up, closes the cupboard door, and with a hinge-moving cry she is born again. The golden colours in the pattern match her pubic hair in the dimmed reflection. And all her other hair humming around her head. She stands and sees a stranger framed in the strange room itself in the strange city. She opens the cupboard, the stranger screams and vanishes. She takes the silk blue skirt, silk lined, steps into it and zips it up, squeals the cupboard shut, walks without a second glance at the stranger into the bathroom where she switches on the mirror light with a white atomic bang and opens the jar of foundation cream. Quickly, mechanically she makes up her face, silk powder, a black line round her eyes, a tinkling drop of water from the tap on to the eyelash brush swiftly left to right on the mascara bar then gently upward on the eyelashes. A comb electric through her hair, a forest put out with a flick of the hand over her shoulders to remove the traces. Crazy earrings balls of fire. She looks at the stranger who is beautiful. The eyes stare out of their black frames, eyes of another that she penetrates and swims in, lips glaring pink and parted as a cave that she enters leaving behind the ringing flowers on her breasts.

Back in the room she steps into her Valentino shoes, picks up her handbag and the key of the room, switches off the light and goes out, calls the lift, enters, down, past the night porter and into the lit street.

The red man stands his legs apart. He is extraordinarily squat and thick with short rectangular legs. And luminous.

She waits.

No car glides by along either street.

The green man walks, equally luminous with equally rectangular legs ending in square green shoes. And yet less squat and thick because he walks.

She goes.

She passes the bookshop without a glance. The silk of the blouse caresses her breasts the silk lining of the skirt her thighs and buttocks as she walks the light long earrings swing from clips that softly bite her lobes. The supple leather of her expensive shoes firmly hugs her heels and toes, leaving the instep bare. The heels knock loudly on the pavement for it to open up.

The red man stands, rectangular legs apart.

She waits.

The streets are empty.

The green man walks light and airy.

She goes.

The street ends in a T-bend formed by an old palace. The curlicues cocoon around the palace gate, take off as butterflies leaving only two cupids with tiny manhoods that rise and grow to the distant ground bass of the city and its high strings that climb and climb. To the right of the gate a blue moon is slashed by a toothpaste smile pointing left. On the right corner of the street the sign shows a black snake at a right angle crossed by a blood-red bar diagonally. The street to the right has a big blood-red eye, gashed across with white teeth. She turns consequently left to cross over, waiting for the green man. When he walks light and airy she crosses past the palace and goes down the left hand street.

The big eyes are blue framed in red lids and crossed by a blood-red bar diagonally.

Consequently she walks on.

Ahead the green man walking beckons. When she reaches him he vanishes, the red man stands, his legs apart, extraordinarily squat and thick. She could never get through to a man so squat and thick.

She waits.

A red car flashes roaring past like a low strafing plane.

The green man walks.

She goes.

The night air is warm and no breeze blows her hair, only her own movements move the silk to caress her skin. She walks slowly, sinuously, to feel the silky touch and the warm air. The luminous red man stands. She waits.

The street is lined with castles upper eyes asleep lower mouths bright wide open full of luminous teeth in lurid garish colours gleaming towers striped pink purple black and coral red blue white rectangles dancing yellow red blue circles witches' brooms sorcerers' apprentice buckets leaping pouring cataracts into the open mouths as the pavements and high walls blow trumpets and beat drums clash cymbals and scream strings higher and higher to sudden echoless silence as if no noise had been.

A white car crawls and even in its slowness stops as a whistling falling bomb. The man bends across to unwind the window on her side. He addresses her in a foreign language.

She looks up at the red man. He is luminously still there, squat and thick, his legs apart.

The driver jerks his head hither leftwards, motioning her into the car. His hair is a forest, his lower face a stubble field.

The green man walks again, light luminous, swift.

She goes, swiftly not sinuously crossing the street in front of the car and he shouts out something through the open window on his side. The voice rings out in gongs, rudeness sounds loving in a foreign language pawing her body with brutal tenderness. He has to wait by the red squat thick man.

She hears him machine-gunning off as she walks on, turns left; into a one-way street in order to meet no stranger walking towards her, only the green man beckoning at the end of the street who becomes the red man standing.

She waits. The golden women in the big illuminated mouth have nothing on. Their breasts are small, their shining bodies poised in stiff ecstatic positions under their bald heads. One still has hair askew, or-ange and stiffly lacquered, stands in profile legs wide apart as if firmly walking oil. The others stand facing her legs wide apart and arms out-stretched in invitation unless offering something they don't have in their shiny golden bodies or saying I can't help it. All the legs have a line round the top of the thigh. There is no pubic hair. The city sings in their veinless bodies, empty heads.

The green man walks, luminous light and swift. He is the safe man.

A white triangular eye framed in red has no dilated pupils or slashed grins but two black arrows one pointing down one up. So she will meet someone after all a woman perhaps walking towards her with the warm air caressing her between the legs. She walks her legs slightly apart to let the warm air in. The silk lining of her skirt is a lover's hands on her thighs her buttocks. The blouse caresses her breasts and she moves her shoulders round as she walks to make the breasts move to the silky touch.

The man lurches out of a doorway. She steps aside. He steps in front of her, legs apart, barring her way. She steps into the street. He does the same. He is squat and thick. She steps back on to the pavement. He follows. He has red hair, a crackling forest fire, he sways, flays out his arms, utters words that gong her body with brutal tenderness all over from the breasts still and high under the silk down to the pubic hair that touches the silk lining as the warm air from the pavement floats up her thighs kissing the open lips like violins. His arms come down in a swift movement to his green corduroy trousers unless blue sea-blue in the sea-blue light unzipped to a white flash of foam that roaring breaks as the sea opens to reveal a coral reef around a huge white peak. It has a pinkish tip like snow in sunset but it can't be snow under the suddenly silent sea in this blue light and it moves, due to the sea water perhaps it swims and two white creatures swim down and surround it or a white octopus and grip it moving up and down with deep quiet grunts. She contemplates the vision and it makes animal noises that paw her body with brutal tenderness as she stands in a tranced stillness smiling kindly waiting for the red-haired man to switch off and turn into the green man walking.

When the white octopus lets go of the white peak it has vanished into the coral reef like a floppy red fish. The foam breaks over the coral reef and the blue green sea zips up again. She inclines her head politely to thank the man for the display, walks past.

At the end of the block the green man flashes on luminous walking her swift and light across the street.

At the next cross road the black right angle slashed by a red diagonal says no right turn. The red man stands. The blue disc shows an arrow pointing left.

It is a one-way street. No man will walk towards her and no man does.

The white disc is framed in red. No entry. An amber light flashes on and off. Cross if safe to do so. There is no green man.

The buildings are not castles with closed eyes and garish mouths but square façades lit up below with Pisan towers of brassieres pink purple coral red flowery panties blue cookers fridges dishwashers yellow plastic buckets red basins carpet sweepers polishers bright-handled floor cleaners. The city is still and silent, only her steps discreetly clock the pavement.

A man in blue or is it green stands on the corner. He is in uniform. He is the safe man.

One could walk miles and miles obeying the code.

Despite his signs she cannot understand his instructions for finding her hotel. He walks with her. How kind, it must be miles and miles on account of the code. But it is round the corner.

She thanks him. He touches his green cap or is it navy blue and walks away.

The hall porter is asleep. The lift opens silently, she steps in. Instructions are printed black on silver metal in a foreign language. She presses button four and feels no movement until the lift stops. She emerges on the carpeted floor in total darkness but for one faint orange star at eye-level which brings on total silent light with a soft short zing at pressure. The key is in her hand as she walks down the corridor. It is marked 41. The door is there. The room exists again in the light switched on.

She shuts the door behind her and locks it from inside. The noise is only of a key turning gently. Puts down her handbag on the dressing table, switches off the light, walks over to the wardrobe. Slowly unzips her silk-lined skirt and folds it carefully over a chair. Stands against the blue light from the street, her hair outlined in it. Walks over to the bed, switches on the bedside lamp and walks back to the wardrobe. In the reflection the gold pattern of her expensive blouse matches her pubic hair and the silver gold halo round her other hair. She unbuttons the blouse, hangs it on the back of the chair. Stands against the bluish gold light outlined in it. Her hands move slowly over her breasts and down, once only. Then she walks naked to the bed, turns down the sheet slips in the cotton sheets soft on her skin turns off the light throws back the sheet and blanket lies fully awake undrugged now naked to the warm night air and the bluish street lighting.

Below the red man stands, the green man walks.

Milton Keynes UK
Ingram Content Group UK Ltd.
UKHW041321240923
429295UK00003B/141